Autobiography of a P

Autobiography of a Pocket Handkerchief

James Fenimore Cooper

ET REMOTISSIMA PROPE

Hesperus Classics

Hesperus Classics
Published by Hesperus Press Limited
4 Rickett Street, London SW6 1RU
www.hesperuspress.com

First published in 1843
First published by Hesperus Press Limited, 2006

Designed and typeset by Fraser Muggeridge studio
Printed in Jordan by Jordan National Press

ISBN: 1-84391-139-6
ISBN13: 978-1-84391-139-5

CONTENTS

FOREWORD

'Who made your t-shirt?' This question, shouted at a demonstration against globalisation in Washington D.C., recently inspired Pietra Rivoli's *The Travels of a T-shirt in the Global Economy: An Economist Examines the Markets, Power, and Politics of World Trade* (2005). Rivoli's clever idea of tracking a single item through the rag trade, from a cotton-field in Texas to a used-clothing bazaar in Africa, also occurred to James Fenimore Cooper, over 160 years ago, when he was the most famous writer in America.

On 22nd September 1842, Cooper wrote testily to his English publisher, 'Your manner of calculating the returns is different from what I had supposed, but I dare say it is suited to the state of the times.' Times were hard in publishing on both sides of the Atlantic. Then as now the industry was highly volatile, booming through cheap paperback sales one minute, crashing the next. Cooper, who had lived well since 1820 off his sea novels and *Leatherstocking Tales*, saw his income shrivel. He felt undervalued – if not actually exploited – by booksellers whose pockets he had lined. Hence that glacial, 'I dare say'.

'A thought flashed on my mind the other day, for a short magazine story,' Cooper's letter continued, 'and I think I shall write it. It will be called *The Autobiography of a Pocket Handkerchief*.' The story that emerged proved Cooper a pioneer in a new domain. Readers of his fiction were familiar with wanderers of the wilderness – Scout, Guide, Pathfinder, Deerslayer, Hawkeye, Long Rifle and Leatherstocking – but an inanimate handkerchief wandering the paths of nineteenth-century commerce was entirely unexpected. Today, experimental fiction narrated by inanimate objects has become *de trop*: the stock-in-trade of creative writing programmes worldwide. But it was not so in Cooper's day. His flash of inspiration was a timely response to new opportunities American magazines (such as *Graham's*) provided for making money and escaping the strictures of traditional novel writing.

'I have ever considered my family as American by origin, European by emigration, and restored to its paternal soil by the mutations and calculations of industry and trade,' the linen handkerchief explains. Cooper imputes consciousness – or 'vegetable clairvoyance' – to the fibres of the *Linum usitatissimum* plant, grown in Connecticut, exported to Europe, replanted in Normandy, then harvested and woven into cambric fine enough to sell in Paris. The conceit of the handkerchief narrator allows Cooper to compare with elegant ease (three decades before Henry James) the manners of the old and new worlds.

Cooper's generation had good reason to compare America with France. Cooper was born in upstate New York in 1789, the year of the French Revolution. His father was a judge and friend of the Federalist Alexander Hamilton. Cooper grew up proud of the American revolutionary achievement and dismayed by France's bloody struggle to establish a republic on the other side of the Atlantic. After his success with *The Last of the Mohicans* (1826), Cooper took his family to live in France, where he saw for himself the countenance of the Duchesse d'Angoulême (daughter of the executed king Louis XVI and queen Marie Antoinette). Cooper wrote, 'I never see this woman without a feeling of commiseration and respect.'

The pocket handkerchief is first intended as a gift for the Duchesse d'Angoulême. It is purchased by a young girl, Adrienne, whose noble grandmother, left impoverished by the Revolution, has been rescued by the Duchesse under the Restoration of the Bourbon monarchy. Before Adrienne can embroider the handkerchief, revolution strikes again in 1830, and she must hope to sell the fruits of her labour to support her ailing grandmother. Adrienne toils night and day to produce the most beautiful handkerchief in France, for which she is paid a pittance. Anticipating Karl Marx, Cooper's story exposes the exploitation of workers in a capitalist economy:

> Those who live on the frivolities of mankind, or, what is the same thing, their luxuries, have two sets of victims to plunder – the consumer, and the real producer, or the operative. This is true where men are employed, but much truer in the case of females.

Little has changed, as Rivoli discovered travelling with her t-shirt.

Contemporary critics in America criticised Cooper heavily for infusing his fiction with social and political argument, but he was undeterred. When the handkerchief is sold for export to the shifty

Colonel Silky, Cooper turns his attention to American manners. Silky is a vulgar fellow: the kind who might inadvertently use the narrator like a lesser handkerchief. However, all goes well, Adrienne's handiwork is smuggled past customs, and is soon for sale at Bobbinet & Co. in New York. Some customers are affronted by such exquisite embroidery on a handkerchief. It would indeed be a disgrace for anyone to blow their nose on it, and for this very reason the item seems in poor taste to the austere sensibilities of America's 'true elite'. Others are entranced by the idea of impressing their peers with a $100 handkerchief. Cooper has fun with the new world's nouveaux riches, yet his satire is fond rather than biting. 'As the rumor that a "three-figure" pocket handkerchief was to be at the ball had preceded my appearance, a general buzz announced my'arrival in the *salle à manger-salons*.' In America, the narrator finds goodness even in the hearts of practising capitalists, and sanguinely reflects: 'I have made some of the warmest and truest-hearted friends in New York that it ever fell to the lot of a pocket handkerchief to enjoy.'

When Alexis de Tocqueville was leaving France to commence his study of America, Cooper was asked to write him a letter of introduction. Cooper happily obliged: de Tocqueville's interests in social and political mores mirrored his own and he greatly admired *Democracy in America* when it was published in 1835 and 1840. Even so, he could not resist the mischievous idea that a pocket handkerchief returning to France 'would have written a book on America, which, while it overlooked many vices and foibles that deserve to be cut up without mercy, would have thrown even de Tocqueville into the shade in the way of political blunders'. Cooper himself certainly never wrote such a book. He did publish in 1838 *The American Democrat: or Hints on the Social and Civic Relations of the United States of America*, but it was quite rightly passed over in favour of de Tocqueville's book as a textbook for schoolchildren. Cooper's real talent was for fiction, not theory, which makes it all the more pleasing to have a keepsake of his political concerns in the guise of a pocket handkerchief.

– Ruth Scurr, 2006

Autobiography of
a Pocket Handkerchief

Certain moral philosophers, with a due disdain of the flimsy foundations of human pride, have shown that every man is equally descended from a million of ancestors, within a given number of generations; thereby demonstrating that no prince exists who does not participate in the blood of some beggar, or any beggar who does not share in the blood of princes. Although favored by a strictly vegetable descent myself, the laws of nature have not permitted me to escape from the influence of this common rule. The earliest accounts I possess of my progenitors represent them as a goodly growth of the *Linum usitatissimum*,[1] divided into a thousand cotemporaneous plants, singularly well conditioned, and remarkable for an equality that renders the production valuable. In this particular, then, I may be said to enjoy a precedency over the Bourbons themselves, who now govern no less than four different states of Europe, and who have sat on thrones these thousand years.

While our family has followed the general human law in the matter just mentioned, it forms a marked exception to the rule that so absolutely controls all of white blood, on this continent, in what relates to immigration and territorial origin. When the American enters on the history of his ancestors, he is driven, after some ten or twelve generations at most, to seek refuge in a country in Europe; whereas exactly the reverse is the case with us, our most remote extraction being American, while our more recent construction and education have taken place in Europe. When I speak of the 'earliest accounts I possess of my progenitors,' authentic information is meant only; for, like other races, we have certain dark legends that might possibly carry us back again to the old world in quest of our estates and privileges. But, in writing this history, it has been my determination from the first, to record nothing but settled truths, and to reject everything in the shape of vague report or unauthenticated anecdote. Under these limitations, I have ever considered my family as American by origin, European by emigration, and restored to its paternal soil by the mutations and calculations of industry and trade.

The glorious family of cotemporaneous plants from which I derive my being, grew in a lovely vale of Connecticut, and quite near to the banks of the celebrated river of the same name. This renders us strictly Yankee in our origin, an extraction of which I find all who enjoy it fond of boasting. It is the only subject of self-felicitation with which I am acquainted that men can indulge in, without awakening the envy of their fellow-creatures; from which I infer it is at least innocent, if not commendable.

We have traditions among us of the enjoyments of our predecessors, as they rioted in the fertility of their cisatlantic field; a happy company of thriving and luxuriant plants. Still, I shall pass them over, merely remarking that a bountiful nature has made such provision for the happiness of all created things as enables each to rejoice in its existence, and to praise, after its fashion and kind, the divine Being to which it owes its creation.

In due time, the field in which my forefathers grew was gathered, the seed winnowed from the chaff and collected in casks, when the whole company was shipped for Ireland. Now occurred one of those chances that decide the fortunes of plants, as well as those of men, giving me a claim to Norman, instead of Milesian[2] descent. The embarkation, or shipment of my progenitors, whichever may be the proper expression, occurred in the height of the last general war, and, for a novelty, it occurred in an English ship. A French privateer captured the vessel on her passage home, the flaxseed was condemned and sold, my ancestors being transferred in a body to the ownership of a certain agriculturist in the neighborhood of Evreux,[3] who dealt largely in such articles. There have been evil disposed vegetables that have seen fit to reproach us with this sale as a stigma on our family history, but I have ever considered it myself as a circumstance of which one has no more reason to be ashamed than a D'Uzès[4] has to blush for the robberies of a baron of the middle ages. Each is an incident in the progress of civilization; the man and the vegetable alike taking the direction pointed out by Providence for the fulfillment of his or its destiny.

Plants have sensation as well as animals. The latter, however, have no consciousness anterior to their physical births, and very little, indeed, for some time afterwards; whereas a different law prevails as respects us; our mental conformation being such as to enable us to refer our moral existence to a period that embraces the experience, reasoning and sentiments of several generations. As respects logical inductions, for instance, the *Linum usitatissimum* draws as largely on the intellectual acquisitions of the various epochs that belonged to the three or four parent stems that preceded it, as on its own. In a word, that accumulated knowledge that man inherits by means of books, imparted and transmitted information, schools, colleges, and universities, we obtain through more subtle agencies that are incorporated with our organic construction, and which form a species of hereditary mesmerism; a vegetable clairvoyance that enables us to see with the eyes, hear with the ears, and digest with the understandings of our predecessors.

Some of the happiest moments of my moral existence were thus obtained, while our family was growing in the fields of Normandy. It happened that a distinguished astronomer selected a beautiful seat, that was placed on the very margin of our position, as a favorite spot for his observations and discourses; from a recollection of the latter of which, in particular, I still derive indescribable satisfaction. It seems as only yesterday – it is in fact fourteen long, long years – that I heard him thus holding forth to his pupils, explaining the marvels of the illimitable void, and rendering clear to my understanding the vast distance that exists between the Being that created all things and the works of his hands. To those who live in the narrow circle of human interests and human feelings, there ever exists, unheeded, almost unnoticed, before their very eyes, the most humbling proofs of their own comparative insignificance in the scale of creation, which, in the midst of their admitted mastery over the earth and all it contains, it would be well for them to consider, if they would obtain just views of what they are and what they were intended to be.

I think I can still hear this learned and devout man – for his soul was filled with devotion to the dread Being that could hold a universe in subjection to His will – dwelling with delight on all the discoveries among the heavenly bodies, that the recent improvements in science and mechanics have enabled the astronomers to make. Fortunately, he gave his discourses somewhat of the progressive character of lectures, leading his listeners on, as it might be step by step, in a way to render all easy to the commonest understanding. Thus it was, I first got accurate notions of the almost inconceivable magnitude of space, to which, indeed, it is probable there are no more positive limits than there are a beginning and an end to eternity! Can these wonders be, I thought – and how pitiful in those who affect to reduce all things to the level of their own powers of comprehension, and their own experience in practice! Let them exercise their sublime and boasted reason, I said to myself, in endeavoring to comprehend infinity in any thing, and we will note the result! If it be in space, we shall find them setting bounds to their illimitable void, until ashamed of the feebleness of their first effort, it is renewed, again and again, only to furnish new proofs of the insufficiency of any of earth, even to bring within the compass of their imaginations truths that all their experiments, inductions, evidence and revelations compel them to admit.

'The moon has no atmosphere,' said our astronomer one day, 'and if inhabited at all, it must be by beings constructed altogether differently from ourselves. Nothing that has life, either animal or vegetable as we know them, can exist without air, and it follows that nothing having life, according to our views of it, can exist in the moon – or, if any thing having life do exist there, it must be under such modifications of all our known facts, as to amount to something like other principles of being.

'One side of that planet feels the genial warmth of the sun for a fortnight, while the other is for the same period without it,' he continued. 'That which feels the sun must be a day, of a heat so intense as to render it insupportable to us, while the opposite side on which the rays of the sun do not fall, must be masses of ice, if water exist there to be congealed. But the moon has no seas, so far as we can ascertain; its surface representing one of strictly volcanic origin, the mountains being numerous to a wonderful degree. Our instruments enable us to perceive craters, with the inner cones so common to all our own volcanos, giving reason to believe in the activity of innumerable burning hills at some remote period. It is scarcely necessary to say that nothing we know could live in the moon under these rapid and extreme transitions of heat and cold, to say nothing of the want of atmospheric air.' I listened to this with wonder, and learned to be satisfied with my station. Of what moment was it to me, in filling the destiny of the *Linum usitatissimum*, whether I grew in a soil a little more or a little less fertile; whether my fibers attained the extremest fineness known to the manufacturer, or fell a little short of this excellence. I was but a speck among a myriad of other things produced by the hand of the Creator, and all to conduce to his own wise ends and unequalled glory. It was my duty to live my time, to be content, and to proclaim the praise of God within the sphere assigned to me. Could men or plants but once elevate their thoughts to the vast scale of creation, it would teach them their own insignificance so plainly, would so unerringly make manifest the futility of complaints, and the immense disparity between time and eternity, as to render the useful lesson of contentment as inevitable as it is important.

I remember that our astronomer, one day, spoke of the nature and magnitude of the sun. The manner that he chose to render clear to the imagination of his hearers some just notions of its size, though so familiar to astronomers, produced a deep and unexpected impression on me. 'Our instruments,' he said, 'are now so perfect and powerful, as to enable us to ascertain many facts of the deepest interest, with near approaches to positive accuracy. The moon being the heavenly body much the nearest to us, of course we see further into its secrets than into those of any other planet. We have calculated its distance from us at 237,000 miles. Of course by doubling this distance, and adding to it the diameter of the earth, we get the diameter of the circle, or orbit, in which the moon moves around the earth. In other words the diameter of this orbit is about 480,000 miles. Now could the sun be brought in contact with this orbit, and had the latter solidity to mark its circumference, it would be found that this circumference would include but a little more than half the surface of one side of the sun, the diameter of which orb is calculated to be 882,000 miles! The sun is one million three hundred and eighty-four thousand four hundred and seventy-two times larger than the earth. Of the substance of the sun it is not so easy to speak. Still it is thought, though it is not certain, that we occasionally see the actual surface of this orb, an advantage we do not possess as respects any other of the heavenly bodies, with the exception of the moon and Mars. The light and warmth of the sun probably exist in its atmosphere, and the spots that are so often seen on this bright orb are supposed to be glimpses of the solid mass of the sun itself, which are occasionally obtained through openings in this atmosphere. At all events, this is the more consistent way of accounting for the appearance of these spots. You will get a better idea of the magnitude of the sidereal system, however, by remembering that, in comparison with it, the distances of our entire solar system are as mere specks. Thus, while our own change of positions is known to embrace an orbit of about 200,000,000 of miles, it is nevertheless so trifling as to produce no apparent change of position in thousands of the fixed stars that are believed to be the suns of other systems. Some conjecture even that all these suns, with their several systems, our own included, revolve around a common centre that is invisible to us, but which is the actual throne of God; the comets that we note and measure being heavenly messengers, as it might be, constantly passing from one of these families of worlds to another.'

I remember that one of the astronomer's pupils asked certain explanations here, touching the planets that it was thought, or rather known, that we could actually see, and those of which the true surfaces were believed to be concealed from us. 'I have told you,' answered the man of science, 'that they are the moon, Mars and the sun. Both Venus and Mercury are nearer to us than Mars, but their relative proximities to the sun have some such effect on their surfaces, as placing an object near a strong light is known to have on its appearance. We are dazzled, to speak popularly, and cannot distinguish minutely. With Mars it is different. If this planet has any atmosphere at all, it is one of no great density, and its orbit being without our own, we can easily trace on its surface the outlines of seas and continents. It is even supposed that the tinge of the latter is that of reddish sandstone, like much of that known in our own world, but more decided in tint, while two brilliant white spots, at its poles, are thought to be light reflected from the snows of those regions, rendered more conspicuous, or disappearing, as they first emerge from a twelvemonths' winter, or melt in a summer of equal duration.'

I could have listened forever to this astronomer, whose lectures so profoundly taught lessons of humility to the created, and which were so replete with silent eulogies on the power of the Creator! What was it to me whether I were a modest plant, of half a cubit in stature, or the proudest oak of the forest – man or vegetable? My duty was clearly to

8

glorify the dread Being who had produced all these marvels, and to fulfill my time in worship, praise and contentment. It mattered not whether my impressions were derived through organs called ears, and were communicated by others called those of speech, or whether each function was performed by means of sensations and agencies too subtle to be detected by ordinary means. It was enough for me that I heard and understood, and felt the goodness and glory of God. I may say that my first great lessons in true philosophy were obtained in these lectures, where I learned to distinguish between the finite and infinite, ceasing to envy any, while I inclined to worship one. The benevolence of Providence is extended to all its creatures, each receiving it in a mode adapted to its own powers of improvement. My destiny being toward a communion with man – or rather with woman – I have ever looked upon these silent communications with the astronomer as so much preparatory schooling, in order that my mind might be prepared for its own *avenir*,[5] and not be blinded by an undue appreciation of the importance of its future associates. I know there are those who will sneer at the supposition of a pocket handkerchief possessing any mind, or *esprit*,[6] at all; but let such have patience and read on, when I hope it will be in my power to demonstrate their error.

2

It is scarcely necessary to dwell on the scenes that occurred between the time I first sprang from the earth and that in which I was 'pulled.' The latter was a melancholy day for me, however, arriving prematurely as regarded my vegetable state, since it was early determined that I was to be spun into threads of unusual fineness. I will only say, here, that my youth was a period of innocent pleasures, during which my chief delight was to exhibit my simple but beautiful flowers, in honor of the hand that gave them birth.

At the proper season, the whole field was laid low, when a scene of hurry and confusion succeeded, to which I find it exceedingly painful to turn in memory. The 'rotting' was the most humiliating part of the process that followed, though, in our case, this was done in clear running water, and the 'crackling' the most uncomfortable.[7] Happily, we were spared the anguish that ordinarily accompanies breaking on the wheel, though we could not be said to have entirely escaped from all its parade. Innocence was our shield, and while we endured some of the disgrace that attaches to mere forms, we had that consolation of which no cruelty or device can deprive the unoffending. Our sorrows were not heightened by the consciousness of undeserving.

There is a period, which occurred between the time of being 'hatchelled'[8] and that of being 'woven,' that it exceeds my powers to delineate. All around me seemed to be in a state of inextricable confusion, out of which order finally appeared in the shape of a piece of cambric, of a quality that brought the workmen far and near to visit it. We were a single family of only twelve, in this rare fabric, among which I remember that I occupied the seventh place in the order of arrangement, and of course in the order of seniority also. When properly folded, and bestowed in a comfortable covering, our time passed pleasantly enough, being removed from all disagreeable sights and smells, and lodged in a place of great security, and indeed of honor, men seldom failing to bestow this attention on their valuables.

It is out of my power to say precisely how long we remained in this passive state in the hands of the manufacturer. It was some weeks, however, if not months; during which our chief communications were on the chances of our future fortunes. Some of our number were ambitious, and would hear to nothing but the probability, nay, the certainty, of our being purchased, as soon as our arrival in Paris should be made known, by the king, in person, and presented to the dauphine, then the first lady in France. The virtues of the Duchesse d'Angoulême[9] were properly appreciated by some of us, while I discovered that others entertained for her any feelings but those of veneration and respect. This diversity of opinion, on a subject of which one would think none of us very well qualified to be judges, was owing to a circumstance of such everyday occurrence as almost to supersede the necessity of telling it, though the narrative would be rendered more complete by an explanation.

It happened, while we lay in the bleaching grounds,[10] that one half of the piece extended into a part of the field that came under the management of a *legitimist*, while the other invaded the dominions of a *liberal*.[11] Neither of these persons had any concern with us, we being under the special superintendence of the head workman, but it was impossible, altogether impossible, to escape the consequences of our *locales*. While the *legitimist* read nothing but the *Moniteur*, the *liberal* read nothing but *Le Temps*, a journal then recently established, in the supposed interests of human freedom. Each of these individuals got a paper at a certain hour, which he read with as much manner as he could command, and with singular perseverance as related to the difficulties to be overcome, to a clientele of bleachers, who reasoned as he reasoned, swore by his oaths, and finally arrived at all his conclusions. The liberals had the best of it as to numbers, and possibly as to wit, the *Moniteur* possessing all the dullness of official dignity under all the dynasties and ministries that have governed France since its establishment. My business, however, is with the effect produced on the pocket hand-kerchiefs, and not with that produced on the laborers. The two extremes were regular *côtés gauches* and *côtés droits*.[12] In other words, all at the right end of the piece became devoted Bourbonists, devoutly believing that princes, who were daily mentioned with so much reverence and respect, could be nothing else but perfect; while the opposite extreme were disposed to think that nothing good could come of Nazareth.[13] In this way, four of our number became decided politicians, not only entertaining a sovereign contempt for the sides they respectively opposed, but beginning to feel sensations approaching to hatred for each other.

The reader will readily understand that these feelings lessened toward the center of the piece, acquiring most intensity at the extremes. I may be said, myself, to have belonged to the *centre gauche*,[14] that being my accidental position in the fabric, when it was a natural consequence to obtain sentiments of this shade. It will be seen, in the end, how prominent were these early impressions, and how far it is worth while for mere pocket handkerchiefs to throw away their time, and permit their feelings to become excited concerning interests that they are certainly not destined to control, and about which, under the most favorable circumstances, they seldom obtain other than very question-able information.

It followed from this state of feeling, that the notion we were about to fall into the hands of the unfortunate daughter of Louis XVI excited considerable commotion and disgust among us. Though very moderate in my political antipathies and predilections, I confess to some excitement in my own case, declaring that if royalty *was* to be my lot, I would prefer not to ascend any higher on the scale than to become the property of that excellent princess, Amélie,[15] who then presided in the Palais Royal, the daughter and sister of a king, but with as little prospects as desires of becoming a queen in her own person. This wish of mine was treated as groveling, and even worse than republican, by the *côté droit* of our piece, while the *côté gauche* sneered at it as manifesting a sneaking regard for station without the spirit to avow it. Both were mistaken, however, no unworthy sentiments entering into my decision. Accident had made me acquainted with the virtues of this estimable woman, and I felt assured that she would treat even a pocket handkerchief kindly. This early opinion has been confirmed by her deportment under very trying and unexpected events. I wish, as I believe she wishes herself, she had never been a queen.

All our family did not aspire as high as royalty. Some looked forward to the glories of a banker's daughter's trousseau – we all understood that our price would be too high for any of the old nobility – while some even fancied that the happiness of traveling in company was reserved for us before we should be called regularly to enter on the duties of life. As we were so closely connected, and on the whole were affectionate as became brothers and sisters, it was the common wish that we might not be separated, but go together into the same wardrobe, let it be foreign or domestic, that of prince or plebeian. There were a few among us who spoke of the Duchesse de Berri[16] as our future mistress, but the notion prevailed that we should so soon pass into the hands of a *femme de chambre*,[17] as to render the selection little desirable. In the end we wisely and philosophically determined to await the result with patience, well knowing that we were altogether in the hands of caprice and fashion.

At length the happy moment arrived when we were to quit the warehouse of the manufacturer. Let what would happen, this was a source of joy, inasmuch as we all knew that we could only vegetate while we continued where we then were, and that too without experiencing the delights of our former position, with good roots in the earth, a genial sun shedding its warmth upon our bosom, and balmy airs fanning our cheeks. We loved change, too, like other people, and had probably seen enough of vegetation, whether figurative or real, to satisfy us. Our departure from Picardie took place in June, 1830, and we reached Paris on the first day of the succeeding month. We went through the formalities of the custom houses, or *barrières*, the same day, and the next morning we were all transferred to a celebrated shop that dealt in articles of our genus. Most of the goods were sent on drays to the *magasin*,[18] but our reputation having preceded us, we were honored with a fiacre, making the journey between the Douane[19] and the shop on the knee of a confidential *commissionaire*.[20]

Great was the satisfaction of our little party as we first drove down through the streets of this capital of Europe – the center of fashion and the abode of elegance. Our natures had adapted themselves to circumstances, and we no longer pined for the luxuries of the *Linum usitatissimum*, but were ready to enter into all the pleasures of our new existence; which we well understood was to be one of pure parade, for no handkerchief of our quality was ever employed on any of the more menial offices of the profession. We might occasionally brush a lady's cheek, or conceal a blush or a smile, but the *usitatissimum*[21] had been left behind us in the fields. The fiacre stopped at the door of a celebrated perfumer, and the *commissionaire*, deeming us of too much value to be left on a carriage seat, took us in her hand while she negotiated a small affair with its mistress. This was our introduction to the pleasant association of sweet odors, of which it was to be our fortune to enjoy in future the most delicate and judicious communion. We knew very well that things of this sort were considered vulgar, unless of the purest quality and used with the tact of good society; but still it was permitted to sprinkle a very little lavender, or exquisite eau de cologne, on a pocket handkerchief. The odor of these two scents, therefore, appeared quite natural to us, and as Mme Savon never allowed any perfume, or *articles* (as these things are technically termed), of inferior quality to pollute her shop, we had no scruples about inhaling the delightful fragrance that breathed in the place. Desirée, the *commissionaire*, could not depart without permitting her friend, Mme Savon, to feast her eyes on the treasure in her own hands. The handkerchiefs were unfolded, amidst a hundred *dieux! ciels!* and *dames!*[22] Our fineness and beauty were extolled in a manner that was perfectly gratifying to the self-esteem of the whole family. Mme Savon imagined that even her perfumes would be more fragrant in such company, and she insisted on letting one drop – a single drop – of her eau de cologne fall on the beautiful texture. I was the happy handkerchief that was thus favored, and long did I riot in that delightful odor, which was just strong enough to fill the air with sensations, rather than impressions of all that is sweet and womanly in the female wardrobe.

3

Notwithstanding this accidental introduction to one of the nicest distinctions of good society, and the general exhilaration that prevailed in our party, I was far from being perfectly happy. To own the truth, I had left my heart in Picardie. I do not say I was in love; I am far from certain that there is any precedent for a pocket handkerchief's being in love at all, and I am quite sure that the sensations I experienced were different from those I have since had frequent occasion to hear described. The circumstances that called them forth were as follows:

The manufactory in which our family was fabricated was formerly known as the Château de la Rocheaimard, and had been the property of the Vicomte de la Rocheaimard previously to the revolution that overturned the throne of Louis XVI[23]. The vicomte and his wife joined the royalists at Coblenz, and the former, with his only son, Adrien de la Rocheaimard, or the Chevalier de la Rocheaimard, as he was usually termed, had joined the allies in their attempted invasion on the soil of France. The vicomte, a *maréchal du camp*,[24] had fallen in battle, but the son escaped, and passed his youth in exile, marrying a few years later, a cousin whose fortunes were at as low an ebb as his own. One child, Adrienne, was the sole issue of this marriage, having been born in the year 1810. Both the parents died before the Restoration, leaving the little girl to the care of her pious grandmother, la vicomtesse, who survived, in a feeble old age, to descant on the former grandeur of her house, and to sigh, in common with so many others, for *le bon vieux temps*.[25] At the Restoration, there was some difficulty in establishing the right of the de la Rocheaimards to their share of the indemnity, a difficulty I never heard explained, but which was probably owing to the circumstance that there was no one in particular to interest themselves in the matter, but an old woman of sixty-five and a little girl of four. Such appellants, unsupported by money, interest, or power, seldom make out a very strong case for reparation of any sort, in this righteous world of ours, and had it not been for the goodness of the dauphine it is probable that the vicomtesse and her granddaughter would have been reduced to downright beggary. But the daughter of the late king got intelligence of the necessities of the two descendants of Crusaders, and a pension of two thousand francs a year was granted, *en attendant*.[26]

Four hundred dollars a year does not appear a large sum, even to the nouveaux riches of America, but it sufficed to give Adrienne and her grandmother a comfortable, and even a respectable subsistence in the provinces. It was impossible for them to inhabit the château, now converted into a workshop and filled with machinery, but lodgings were procured in its immediate vicinity. Here Mme de la Rocheaimard whiled away the close of a varied and troubled life, if not in absolute peace, still not in absolute misery, while her granddaughter grew into young womanhood, a miracle of goodness and pious devotion to her sole surviving parent. The strength of the family tie in France, and its comparative weakness in America, has been the subject of frequent comment among travelers. I do not know that all that has been said is rigidly just, but I am inclined to think that much of it is, and, as I am now writing to Americans, and of French people, I see no particular reason why the fact should be concealed. Respect for years, deference to the authors of their being, and submission to parental authority are inculcated equally by the morals and the laws of France. The *conseilles de famille*[27] is a beautiful and wise provision of the national code, and aids greatly in maintaining that system of patriarchal rule that lies at the foundation of the whole social structure. Alas! in the case of the excellent Adrienne, this *conseille de famille* was easily assembled, and possessed perfect unanimity. The wars, the guillotine and exile had reduced it to two, one of which was despotic in her government, so far as theory was concerned at least, possibly, at times, a little so in practice. Still Adrienne, on the whole, grew up tolerably happy. She was taught most that is suitable for a gentlewoman, without being crammed with superfluous accomplishments, and, aided by the good *curé*,[28] a man who remembered her grandfather, had both polished and stored her mind. Her manners were of the excellent tone that distinguished the good society of Paris before the revolution, being natural, quiet, simple and considerate. She seldom laughed, I fear; but her smiles were sweetness and benevolence itself.

The bleaching grounds of our manufactory were in the old park of the château. Thither Mme de la Rocheaimard was fond of coming in the fine mornings of June, for many of the roses and lovely Persian lilacs that once abounded there still remained. I first saw Adrienne in one of these visits, the quality of our little family circle attracting her attention. One of the bleachers, indeed, was an old servant of the vicomte's, and it was a source of pleasure to him to point out any thing to the ladies that he thought might prove interesting. This was the man who so diligently read the *Moniteur*, giving a religious credence to all it contained. He fancied no hand so worthy to hold fabrics of such exquisite fineness as that of Mlle Adrienne, and it was through his assiduity that I had the honor of being first placed within the gentle pressure of her beautiful little fingers. This occurred about a month before our departure for Paris.

Adrienne de la Rocheaimard was then just twenty. Her beauty was of a character that is not common in France; but which, when it does exist, is nowhere surpassed. She was slight and delicate in person, of fair hair and complexion, and with the meekest and most dove-like blue eyes I ever saw in a female face. Her smile, too, was of so winning and gentle a nature, as to announce a disposition pregnant with all the affections. Still it was well understood that Adrienne was not likely to marry, her birth raising her above all intentions of connecting her ancient name with mere gold, while her poverty placed an almost insuperable barrier between her and most of the impoverished young men of rank whom she occasionally saw. Even the power of the dauphine was not suffi-cient to provide Adrienne de la Rocheaimard with a suitable husband. But of this the charming girl never thought; she lived more for her

16

grandmother than for herself, and so long as that venerated relative, almost the only one that remained to her on earth, did not suffer or repine, she herself could be comparatively happy.

'*Dans le bon vieux temps*,' said the vicomtesse, examining me through her spectacles, and addressing Georges, who stood, hat in hand, to hearken to her wisdom; '*dans le bon vieux temps, mon ami*,[29] the ladies of the château did not want for these things. There were six dozen in my *corbeille*,[30] that were almost as fine as this; as for the trousseau, I believe it had twice the number, but very little inferior.'

'I remember that madame,' Georges always gave his old mistress this title of honor, 'kept many of the beautiful garments of her trousseau untouched, down to the melancholy period of the revolution.'

'It has been a mine of wealth to me, Georges, on behalf of that dear child. You may remember that this trousseau was kept in the old armoire, on the right-hand side of the little door of my dressing room – '

'Madame la Vicomtesse will have the goodness to pardon me – it was on the *left*-hand side of the room – Monsieur's medals were kept in the opposite armoire.'

'Our good Georges is right, Adrienne! – he has a memory! Your grandfather insisted on keeping his medals in my dressing room, as he says. Well, Monsieur Georges, left or right, *there* I left the remains of my trousseau when I fled from France, and there I found it untouched on my return. The manufactory had saved the château, and the manufacturers had spared my wardrobe. Its sale, and its materials, have done much toward rendering that dear child respectable and well clad, since our return.'

I thought the slight color that usually adorned the fair oval cheeks of Adrienne deepened a little at this remark, and I certainly felt a little tremor in the hand that held me; but it could not have been shame, as the sweet girl often alluded to her poverty in a way so simple and natural, as to prove that she had no false feelings on that subject. And why should she? Poverty ordinarily causes no such sensations to those who are conscious of possessing advantages of an order superior to wealth, and surely a well-educated, well-born, virtuous girl need not have blushed because estates were torn from her parents by a political convulsion that had overturned an ancient and powerful throne.

4

From this time, the charming Adrienne frequently visited the bleaching grounds, always accompanied by her grandmother. The presence of Georges was an excuse, but to watch the improvement in our appearance was the reason. Never before had Adrienne seen a fabric as beautiful as our own, and, as I afterwards discovered, she was laying by a few francs with the intention of purchasing the piece, and of working and ornamenting the handkerchiefs, in order to present them to her benefactress, the dauphine. Madame de la Rocheaimard was pleased with this project; it was becoming in a de la Rocheaimard, and they soon began to speak of it openly in their visits. Fifteen or twenty napoleons[31] might do it, and the remains of the recovered trousseau would still produce that sum. It is probable this intention would have been carried out, but for a severe illness that attacked the dear girl, during which her life was even despaired of. I had the happiness of hearing of her gradual recovery, however, before we commenced our journey, though no more was said of the purchase. Perhaps it was as well as it was; for, by this time, such a feeling existed in our extreme *côté gauche*, that it may be questioned if the handkerchiefs of that end of the piece would have behaved themselves in the wardrobe of the dauphine with the discretion and prudence that are expected from every thing around the person of a princess of her exalted rank and excellent character. It is true, none of us understood the questions at issue, but that only made the matter worse; the violence of all dissensions being very generally in proportion to the ignorance and consequent confidence of the disputants.

I could not but remember Adrienne, as the *commissionaire* laid us down before the eyes of the wife of the head of the firm, in the rue de — . We were carefully examined, and pronounced '*parfaits*;'[32] still it was not in the sweet tones, and with the sweeter smiles of the polished and gentle girl we had left in Picardie. There was a sentiment in *her* admiration that touched all our hearts, even to the most exaggerated republican among us, for she seemed to go deeper in her examination of merits than the mere texture and price. She saw her offering in our beauty, the benevolence of the dauphine in our softness, her own gratitude in our exquisite fineness, and princely munificence in our delicacy. In a word, she could enter into the sentiment of a pocket handkerchief. Alas! how different was the estimation in which we were held by Desirée and her employers. With them, it was purely a question of francs, and we had not been in the *magasin* five minutes, when there was a lively dispute whether we were to be put at a certain number of napoleons, or one napoleon more. A good deal was said about Mme la Duchesse, and I found that it was expected that a certain lady of that rank, one who had enjoyed the extraordinary luck of retaining her fortune, being of an old and historical family, and who was at the head of fashion in the *faubourg*,[33] would become the purchaser. At all events, it was determined no one should see us until this lady returned to town, she being at the moment at Rosny, with Madame,[34] whence she was expected to accompany that princess to Dieppe, to come back to her hotel, in the rue de Bourbon, about the last of October. Here, then, were we doomed to three months of total seclusion in the heart of the gayest capital of Europe. It was useless to repine, and we determined among ourselves to exercise patience in the best manner we could.

Accordingly, we were safely deposited in a particular drawer, along with a few other favorite *articles*, which, like our family, were reserved for the eyes of certain distinguished but absent customers. These *specialités* in trade are of frequent occurrence in Paris, and form a pleasant bond of union between the buyer and seller, which gives a particular zest to this sort of commerce, and not unfrequently a particular value to goods. To see that which no one else has seen, and to own that which no one else can own, are equally agreeable, and delightfully exclusive. All minds that do not possess the natural sources of exclusion, are fond of creating them by means of a subordinate and more artificial character.

On the whole, I think we enjoyed our new situation, rather than otherwise. The drawer was never opened, it is true, but that next it was in constant use, and certain crevices beneath the counter enabled us to see a little, and to hear more, of what passed in the *magasin*. We were in a part of the shop most frequented by ladies, and we overheard a few tête-à-têtes that were not without amusement. These generally related to *cancans*[35]. Paris is a town in which *cancans* do not usually flourish, their proper theater being provincial and trading places, beyond a question; still there are *cancans* at Paris; for all sorts of persons frequent that center of civilization. The only difference is, that in the social pictures offered by what are called cities, the *cancans* are in the strongest light, and in the most conspicuous of the grouping, whereas in Paris they are kept in shadow, and in the background. Still there are *cancans* at Paris; and *cancans* we overheard, and precisely in the manner I have related. Did pretty ladies remember that pocket handkerchiefs have ears, they might possibly have more reserve in the indulgence of this extraordinary propensity.

We had been near a month in the drawer, when I recognized a female voice near us, that I had often heard of late, speaking in a confident and decided tone, and making allusions that showed she belonged to the court. I presume her position there was not of the most exalted kind, yet it was sufficiently so to qualify her, in her own estimation, to talk politics. '*Les ordonnances*'[36] were in her mouth constantly, and it was easy to perceive that she attached the greatest importance to these ordinances, whatever they were, and fancied a political millennium was near. The shop was frequented less than usual that day; the next it was worse still, in the way of business, and the clerks began to talk loud, also, about *les ordonnances*. The following morning neither windows nor doors were opened, and we passed a gloomy time of uncertainty and conjecture. There were ominous sounds in the streets. Some of us thought we heard the roar of distant artillery. At length the master and mistress appeared by themselves in the shop; money and papers were secured, and the female was just retiring to an inner room, when she suddenly came back to the counter, opened our drawer, seized us with no very reverent hands, and, the next thing we knew, the whole twelve of us were thrust into a trunk upstairs, and buried in Egyptian darkness. From that moment all traces of what was occurring in the streets of Paris were lost to us. After all, it is not so very disagreeable to be only a pocket handkerchief in a revolution.

Our imprisonment lasted until the following December. As our feelings had become excited on the questions of the day, as well as those of other irrational beings around us, we might have passed a most uncomfortable time in the trunk, but for one circumstance. So great had been the hurry of our mistress in thus shutting us up, that we had been crammed in in a way to leave it impossible to say which was the *côté droit*, and which the *côté gauche*. Thus completely deranged as parties, we took to discussing philosophical matters in general, an occupation well adapted to a situation that required so great an exercise of discretion.

One day, when we least expected so great a change, our mistress came in person, searched several chests, trunks and drawers, and finally discovered us where she had laid us, with her own hands, near four months before. It seems that, in her hurry and fright, she had actually forgotten in what nook we had been concealed. We were smoothed with care, our political order reestablished, and then we were taken below and restored to the dignity of the select circle in the drawer already mentioned. This was like removing to a fashionable square, or living in a *beau quartier*[37] of a capital. It was even better than removing from East Broadway into bona fide, real, unequaled, league-long, eighty feet wide, Broadway!

We now had an opportunity of learning some of the great events that had recently occurred in France, and which still troubled Europe. The Bourbons were again dethroned, as it was termed, and another Bourbon seated in their place. It would seem *il y a Bourbon et Bourbon*.[38] The result has since shown that 'what is bred in the bone will break out in the flesh.' Commerce was at a standstill; our master passed half his time under arms, as a national guard, in order to keep the revolutionists from revolutionizing the revolution. The great families had laid aside their liveries; some of them their coaches; most of them their arms. Pocket handkerchiefs of *our* caliber would be thought decidedly aristocratic; and aristocracy in Paris, just at that moment, was almost in as bad odor as it is in America, where it ranks as an eighth deadly sin, though no one seems to know precisely what it means. In the latter country, an honest development of democracy is certain to be stigmatized as tainted with this crime. No governor would dare to pardon it.

The groans over the state of trade were loud and deep among those who lived by its innocent arts. Still, the holidays were near, and hope revived. If revolutionized Paris would not buy as the *jour de l'an*[39] approached, Paris must have a new dynasty. The police foresaw this, and it ceased to agitate, in order to bring the republicans into discredit; men must eat, and trade was permitted to revive a little. Alas! how little do they who vote, know *why* they vote, or they who dye their hands in the blood of their kind, why the deed has been done!

The duchesse had not returned to Paris, neither had she emigrated. Like most of the high nobility, who rightly enough believed that primogeniture and birth were of the last importance to *them*, she preferred to show her distaste for the present order of things, by which the youngest prince of a numerous family had been put upon the throne of the oldest, by remaining at her château. All expectations of selling us to *her* were abandoned, and we were thrown fairly into the market, on the great principle of liberty and equality. This was as became a republican reign.

Our prospects were varied daily. The dauphine, Madame, and all the de Rochefoucaulds, de la Tremouilles, de Grammonts, de Rohans, de Crillons, &c. &c., were out of the question. The royal family were in England, the Orleans branch excepted, and the high nobility were very generally on their 'high ropes,' or, *à bouder*.[40] As for the bankers, their reign had not yet fairly commenced. Previously to July, 1830, this estimable class of citizens had not dared to indulge their native tastes for extravagance and parade, the grave dignity and high breeding of a very ancient but impoverished nobility holding them in some restraint; and, then, *their* fortunes were still uncertain; the funds were not firm, and even the honorable and worthy Jacques Lafitte,[41] a man to ennoble any calling, was shaking in credit. Had we been brought into the market a twelvemonth later, there is no question that we should have been caught up within a week, by the wife or daughter of some of the operatives at the Bourse[42].

As it was, however, we enjoyed ample leisure for observation and thought. Again and again were we shown to those who, it was thought, could not fail to yield to our beauty, but no one would purchase. All appeared to eschew aristocracy, even in their pocket handkerchiefs. The day the fleurs de lys were cut out of the medallions of the treasury, and the king laid down his arms, I thought our mistress would have had the hysterics on our account. Little did she understand human nature, for the nouveaux riches, who are as certain to succeed an old and displaced class of superiors, as hungry flies to follow flies with full bellies, would have been much more apt to run into extravagance and folly, than persons always accustomed to money, and who did not depend on its exhibition for their importance. A day of deliverance, notwithstanding, was at hand, which to me seemed like the bridal of a girl dying to rush into the dissipations of society.

5

The holidays were over, without there being any material revival of trade, when my deliverance unexpectedly occurred. It was in February, and I do believe our mistress had abandoned the expectation of dis-posing of us that season, when I heard a gentle voice speaking near the counter, one day, in tones that struck me as familiar. It was a female, of course, and her inquiries were about a piece of cambric handkerchiefs, which she said had been sent to this shop from a manufactory in Picardie. There was nothing of the customary alertness in the manner of our mistress, and, to my surprise, she even showed the customer one or two pieces of much inferior quality, before we were produced. The moment I got into the light, however, I recognized the beautifully turned form and sweet face of Adrienne de la Rocheaimard. The poor girl was paler and thinner than when I had last seen her, doubtless, I thought, the effects of her late illness; but I could not conceal from myself the unpleasant fact that she was much less expensively clad. I say less expensively clad, though the expression is scarcely just, for I had never seen her in attire that could properly be called expensive at all; and, yet, the term mean would be equally inapplicable to her present appearance. It might be better to say that, relieved by a faultless, even a fastidious neatness and grace, there was an air of severe, perhaps of pinched economy in her present attire. This it was that had pre-vented our mistress from showing her fabrics as fine as we, on the first demand. Still I thought there was a slight flush on the cheek of the poor girl, and a faint smile on her features, as she instantly recognized us for old acquaintances. For one, I own I was delighted at finding her soft fingers again brushing over my own exquisite surface, feeling as if one had been expressly designed for the other. Then Adrienne hesitated; she appeared desirous of speaking, and yet abashed. Her color went and came, until a deep rosy blush settled on each cheek, and her tongue found utterance.

'Would it suit you, madame,' she asked, as if dreading a repulse, 'to part with one of these?'

'Your pardon, mademoiselle; handkerchiefs of this quality are seldom sold singly.'

'I feared as much – and yet I have occasion for only *one*. It is to be worked – if it – '

The words came slowly, and they were spoken with difficulty. At that last uttered, the sound of the sweet girl's voice died entirely away. I fear it was the dullness of trade, rather than any considerations of benevolence, that induced our mistress to depart from her rule.

'The price of each handkerchief is five and twenty francs, mademoiselle – ' she had offered the day before to sell us to the wife of one of the richest *agents de change*[43] in Paris, at a napoleon a piece – 'the price is five and twenty francs, if you take the dozen, but as you appear to wish only *one*, rather than not oblige you, it may be had for eight and twenty.'

There was a strange mixture of sorrow and delight in the countenance of Adrienne; but she did not hesitate, and, attracted by the odor of the eau de cologne, she instantly pointed me out as the handkerchief she selected. Our mistress passed her scissors between me and my neighbor of the *côté gauche*, and then she seemed instantly to regret her own precipitation. Before making the final separation from the piece, she delivered herself of her doubts.

'It is worth another franc, mademoiselle,' she said, 'to cut a handkerchief from the *center* of the piece.'

The pain of Adrienne was now too manifest for concealment. That she ardently desired the handkerchief was beyond dispute, and yet there existed some evident obstacle to her wishes.

'I fear I have not so much money with me, madame,' she said, pale as death, for all sense of shame was lost in intense apprehension. Still her trembling hands did their duty, and her purse was produced. A gold napoleon promised well, but it had no fellow. Seven more francs appeared in single pieces. Then two ten-sous[44] were produced; after which nothing remained but copper. The purse was emptied, and the reticule rummaged, the whole amounting to just twenty-eight francs seven sous.

'I have no more, madame,' said Adrienne, in a faint voice.

The woman, who had been trained in the school of suspicion, looked intently at the other, for an instant, and then she swept the money into her drawer, content with having extorted from this poor girl more than she would have dared to ask of the wife of the *agent de change*. Adrienne took me up and glided from the shop, as if she feared her dear bought prize would yet be torn from her. I confess my own delight was so great that I did not fully appreciate, at the time, all the hardship of the case. It was enough to be liberated, to get into the fresh air, to be about to fulfill my proper destiny. I was tired of that sort of vegetation in which I neither grew, nor was watered by tears; nor could I see those stars on which I so much doted, and from which I had learned a wisdom so profound. The politics, too, were rendering our family unpleasant; the *côté droit* was becoming supercilious – it had always been illogical; while the *côté gauche* was just beginning to discover that it had made a revolution for other people. Then it was happiness itself to be with Adrienne, and when I felt the dear girl pressing me to her heart, by an act of volition of which pocket handkerchiefs are little suspected, I threw up a fold of my gossamer-like texture, as if the air wafted me, and brushed the first tear of happiness from her eye that she had shed in months.

The reader may be certain that my imagination was all alive to conjecture the circumstances that had brought Adrienne de la Rocheaimard to Paris, and why she had been so assiduous in searching me out, in particular. Could it be that the grateful girl still intended to make her offering to the Duchesse d'Angoulême? Ah! no – that princess was in exile; while her sister was forming weak plots on behalf of her son, which a double treachery was about to defeat. I have already hinted that pocket handkerchiefs do not receive and communicate ideas, by means of the organs in use among human beings. They possess a clairvoyance that is always available under favorable circumstances. In their case the mesmeritic trance may be said to be ever in existence, while in the performance of their proper functions. It is only while crowded into bales, or thrust into drawers for the vulgar purposes of trade, that this instinct is dormant, a beneficent nature scorning to exercise her benevolence for any but legitimate objects. I now mean legitimacy as connected with cause and effect, and nothing political or dynastic.

By virtue of this power, I had not long been held in the soft hand of Adrienne, or pressed against her beating heart, without becoming the master of all her thoughts, as well as her various causes of hope and fear. This knowledge did not burst upon me at once, it is true, as is pretended to be the case with certain somnambules, for with me there is no empiricism – everything proceeds from cause to effect, and a little time, with some progressive steps, was necessary to make me fully acquainted with the whole. The simplest things became the first apparent, and others followed by a species of magnetic induction, which I cannot now stop to explain. When this tale is told, I propose to lecture on the subject, to which all the editors in the country will receive the usual free tickets, when the world cannot fail of knowing quite as much, at least, as these meritorious public servants.

The first fact that I learned, was the very important one that the vicomtesse had lost all her usual means of support by the late revolution, and the consequent exile of the dauphine. This blow, so terrible to the grandmother and her dependent child, had occurred, too, most inopportunely, as to time. A half year's pension was nearly due at the moment the great change occurred, and the day of payment arrived and passed, leaving these two females literally without twenty francs. Had it not been for the remains of the trousseau, both must have begged, or perished of want. The crisis called for decision, and fortunately the old lady, who had already witnessed so many vicissitudes, had still sufficient energy to direct their proceedings. Paris was the best place in which to dispose of her effects, and thither she and Adrienne came, without a moment's delay. The shops were first tried, but the shops, in the autumn of 1830, offered indifferent resources for the seller. Valuable effects were there daily sold for a twentieth part of their original cost, and the vicomtesse saw her little stores diminish daily; for the Mont de Piété[45] was obliged to regulate its own proceedings by the received current values of the day. Old age, vexation, and this last most cruel blow, did not fail of effecting that which might have been foreseen. The vicomtesse sunk under this accumulation of misfortunes, and became bedridden, helpless, and querulous. Every thing now devolved on the timid, gentle, unpracticed Adrienne. All females of her condition, in countries advanced in civilization like France, look to the resource of imparting a portion of what they themselves have acquired, to others of their own sex, in moments of urgent necessity. The possibility of Adrienne's being compelled to become a governess, or a companion, had long been kept in view, but the situation of Mme de la Rocheaimard forbade any attempt of the sort, for the moment, had the state of the country rendered it at all probable that a situation could have been procured. On this fearful exigency, Adrienne had aroused all her energies, and gone deliberately into the consideration of her circumstances.

Poverty had compelled Mme de la Rocheaimard to seek the cheapest respectable lodgings she could find on reaching town. In anticipation of a long residence, and, for the consideration of a considerable abatement in price, she had fortunately paid six months' rent in advance, thus removing from Adrienne the apprehension of having no place in which to cover her head, for some time to come. These lodgings were in an entresol of the Place Royale, a perfectly reputable and private part of the town, and in many respects were highly eligible. Many of the menial offices, too, were to be performed by the wife of the porter, according to the bargain, leaving to poor Adrienne, however, all the care of her grandmother, whose room she seldom quitted, the duties of nurse and cook, and the still more important task of finding the means of subsistence.

For quite a month the poor desolate girl contrived to provide for her grandmother's necessities, by disposing of the different articles of the trousseau. This store was now nearly exhausted, and she had found a milliner who gave her a miserable pittance for toiling with her needle eight or ten hours each day. Adrienne had not lost a moment, but had begun this system of ill-requited industry long before her money was exhausted. She foresaw that her grandmother must die, and the great object of her present existence was to provide for the few remaining wants of this only relative during the brief time she had yet to live, and to give her decent and Christian burial. Of her own future lot, the poor girl thought as little as possible, though fearful glimpses would obtrude themselves on her uneasy imagination. At first she had employed a physician; but her means could not pay for his visits, nor did the situation of her grandmother render them very necessary. He promised to call occasionally without fee, and, for a short time, he kept his word, but his benevolence soon wearied of performing offices that really were not required. By the end of a month, Adrienne saw him no more.

As long as her daily toil seemed to supply her own little wants, Adrienne was content to watch on, weep on, pray on, in waiting for the moment she so much dreaded; that which was to sever the last tie she appeared to possess on earth. It is true she had a few very distant relatives, but they had emigrated to America, at the commencement of the revolution of 1789, and all trace of them had long been lost. In point of fact, the men were dead, and the females were grandmothers with English names, and were almost ignorant of any such persons as the de la Rocheaimards. From these Adrienne had nothing to expect. To her, they were as beings in another planet. But the trousseau was nearly exhausted, and the stock of ready money was reduced to a single napoleon, and a little change. It was absolutely necessary to decide on some new scheme for a temporary subsistence, and that without delay.

Among the valuables of the trousseau was a piece of exquisite lace, that had never been even worn. The vicomtesse had a pride in looking at it, for it showed the traces of her former wealth and magnificence, and she would never consent to part with it. Adrienne had carried it once to her employer, the milliner, with the intention of disposing of it, but the price offered was so greatly below what she knew to be the true value, that she would not sell it. Her own wardrobe, however, was going fast, nothing disposable remained of her grandmother's, and this piece of lace must be turned to account in some way. While reflecting on these dire necessities, Adrienne remembered our family. She knew to what shop we had been sent in Paris, and she now determined to purchase one of us, to bestow on the handkerchief selected some of her own beautiful needlework, to trim it with this lace, and, by the sale, to raise a sum sufficient for all her grandmother's earthly wants.

Generous souls are usually ardent. Their hopes keep pace with their wishes, and, as Adrienne had heard that twenty napoleons were

28

sometimes paid by the wealthy for a single pocket handkerchief, when thus decorated, she saw a little treasure in reserve, before her mind's eye.

'I can do the work in two months,' she said to herself, 'by taking the time I have used for exercise, and by severe economy; by eating less myself, and working harder, we can make out to live that time on what we have.'

This was the secret of my purchase, and the true reason why this lovely girl had literally expended her last sou in making it. The cost had materially exceeded her expectations, and she could not return home without disposing of some article she had in her reticule, to supply the vacuum left in her purse. There would be nothing ready for the milliner, under two or three days, and there was little in the lodgings to meet the necessities of her grandmother. Adrienne had taken her way along the quays, delighted with her acquisition, and was far from the Mont de Piété before this indispensable duty occurred to her mind. She then began to look about her for a shop in which she might dispose of something for the moment. Luckily she was the mistress of a gold thimble, which had been presented to her by her grandmother, as her very last birthday present. It was painful for her to part with it, but, as it was to supply the wants of that very parent, the sacrifice cost her less than might otherwise have been the case. Its price had been a napoleon, and a napoleon, just then, was a mint of money in her eyes. Besides, she had a silver thimble at home, and a brass one would do for her work.

Adrienne's necessities had made her acquainted with several jewelers' shops. To one of these she now proceeded, and, first observing through the window that no person was in but one of her own sex, the silversmith's wife, she entered with the greater confidence and alacrity.

'Madame,' she said, in timid tones, for want had not yet made Adrienne bold or coarse, 'I have a thimble to dispose of – could you be induced to buy it?'

The woman took the thimble and examined it, weighed it, and submitted its metal to the test of the touchstone. It was a pretty thimble, though small, or it would not have fitted Adrienne's finger. This fact struck the woman of the shop, and she cast a suspicious glance at

Adrienne's hand, the whiteness and size of which, however, satisfied her that the thimble had not been stolen.

'What do you expect to receive for this thimble, mademoiselle?' asked the woman, coldly.

'It cost a napoleon, madame, and was made expressly for myself.'

'You do not expect to sell it at what it cost?' was the dry answer.

'Perhaps not, madame – I suppose you will look for a profit in selling it again. I wish you to name the price.'

This was said because the delicate ever shrink from affixing a value to the time and services of others. Adrienne was afraid she might unintentionally deprive the other of a portion of her just gains. The woman understood by the timidity and undecided manner of the applicant that she had a very unpracticed being to deal with, and she was emboldened to act accordingly. First taking another look at the pretty little hand and fingers, to make certain the thimble might not be reclaimed, when satisfied that it really belonged to her who wished to dispose of it, she ventured to answer.

'In such times as we had before these vile republicans drove all the strangers from Paris, and when our commerce was good,' she said, 'I might have offered seven francs and a half for that thimble; but, as things are now, the last sou I can think of giving is five francs.'

'The gold is very good, madame,' Adrienne observed, in a voice half-choked; 'they told my grandmother the metal alone was worth thirteen.'

'Perhaps, mademoiselle, they might give that much at the mint, for there they coin money; but, in this shop, no one will give more than five francs for that thimble.'

Had Adrienne been longer in communion with a cold and heartless world, she would not have submitted to this piece of selfish extortion; but, inexperienced, and half frightened by the woman's manner, she begged the pittance offered as a boon, dropped her thimble, and made a hasty retreat. When the poor girl reached the street, she began to reflect on what she had done. Five francs would scarcely support her grandmother a week, with even the wood and wine she had on hand, and she had no more gold thimbles to sacrifice. A heavy sigh broke from her bosom, and tears stood in her eyes. But she was wanted at home, and had not the leisure to reflect on her own mistake.

6

Occupation is a blessed relief to the miserable. Of all the ingenious modes of torture that have ever been invented, that of solitary confinement is probably the most cruel – the mind feeding on itself with the rapacity of a cormorant, when the conscience quickens its activity and feeds its longings. Happily for Adrienne, she had too many positive cares to be enabled to waste many minutes either in retrospection, or in endeavors to conjecture the future. Far – far more happily for herself, her conscience was clear, for never had a purer mind, or a gentler spirit dwelt in female breast. Still she could blame her own oversight, and it was days before her self-upbraidings, for thus trifling with what she conceived to be the resources of her beloved grandmother, were driven from her thoughts by the pressure of other and greater ills.

Were I to last a thousand years, and rise to the dignity of being the handkerchief that the Grand Turk is said to toss toward his favorite, I could not forget the interest with which I accompanied Adrienne to the door of her little apartment, in the entresol. She was in the habit of hiring little Nathalie, the porter's daughter, to remain with her grandmother during her own necessary but brief absences, and this girl was found at the entrance, eager to be relieved.

'Has my grandmother asked for me, Nathalie?' demanded Adrienne, anxiously, the moment they met.

'*Non*, mademoiselle; madame has done nothing but sleep, and I was getting *so* tired!'

The sou was given, and the porter's daughter disappeared, leaving Adrienne alone in the antechamber. The furniture of this little apartment was very respectable, for Mme de la Rocheaimard, besides paying a pretty fair rent, had hired it just after the revolution, when the prices had fallen quite half, and the place had, by no means, the appearance of that poverty that actually reigned within. Adrienne went through the antechamber, which served also as a *salle à manger*,[46] and passed a small saloon, into the bedchamber of her parent. Here her mind was relieved by finding all right. She gave her grandmother some nourishment, inquired tenderly as to her wishes, executed several little necessary offices, and then sat down to work for her own daily bread, every moment being precious to one so situated. I expected to be examined – perhaps caressed, fondled, or praised, but no such attention awaited me. Adrienne had arranged everything in her own mind, and I was to be produced only at those extra hours in the morning, when she had been accustomed to take exercise in the open air. For the moment I was laid aside, though in a place that enabled me to be a witness of all that occurred. The day passed in patient toil, on the part of the poor girl, the only relief she enjoyed being those moments when she was called on to attend to the wants of her grandmother. A light potage, with a few grapes and bread, composed her dinner; even of these I observed that she laid aside nearly half for the succeeding day, doubts of her having the means of supporting her parent until the handkerchief was completed beginning to beset her mind. It was these painful and obtrusive doubts that most distressed the dear girl now, for the expectation of reaping a reward comparatively brilliant, from the ingenious device to repair her means on which she had fallen, was strong within her. Poor child! her misgivings were the overflowings of a tender heart, while her hopes partook of the sanguine character of youth and inexperience!

My turn came the following morning. It was now spring, and this is a season of natural delights at Paris. We were already in April, and the flowers had begun to shed their fragrance on the air, and to brighten the aspect of the public gardens. Madame de la Rocheaimard usually slept the soundest at this hour, and, hitherto, Adrienne had not hesitated to leave her, while she went herself to the nearest public promenade, to breathe the pure air and to gain strength for the day. In future, she was to deny herself this sweet gratification. It was such a sacrifice, as the innocent and virtuous, and I may add the tasteful, who are cooped up amid the unnatural restraints of a town, will best know how to appreciate. Still it was made without a murmur, though not without a sigh.

When Adrienne laid me on the frame where I was to be ornamented by her own pretty hands, she regarded me with a look of delight, nay, even of affection, that I shall never forget. As yet she felt none of the malign consequences of the self-denial she was about to exert. If not blooming, her cheeks still retained some of their native color, and her eye, thoughtful and even sad, was not yet anxious and sunken. She was pleased with her purchase, and she contemplated prodigies in the way of results. Adrienne was unusually skillful with the needle, and her taste had been so highly cultivated, as to make her a perfect mistress of all the proprieties of patterns. At the time it was thought of making an offering of all our family to the dauphine, the idea of working the handkerchiefs was entertained, and some designs of exquisite beauty and neatness had been prepared. They were not simple, vulgar, unmeaning ornaments, such as the uncultivated seize upon with avidity on account of their florid appearance, but well-devised drawings, which were replete with taste and thought, and afforded some apology for the otherwise sense-less luxury contemplated, by aiding in refining the imagination, and cultivating the intellect. She had chosen one of the simplest and most beautiful of these designs, intending to transfer it to my face, by means of the needle.

The first stitch was made just as the clocks were striking the hour of five, on the morning of 14th April, 1831. The last was drawn that day two months, precisely as the same clocks struck twelve. For four hours Adrienne sat bending over her toil, deeply engrossed in the occupation, and flattering herself with the fruits of her success. I learned much of the excellent child's true character in these brief hours. Her mind wandered over her hopes and fears, recurring to her other labors, and the prices she received for occupations so wearying and slavish. By the milliner, she was paid merely as a common sewing-girl, though her neatness, skill and taste might well have entitled her to double wages. A franc a day was the usual price for girls of an inferior caste, and out of this they were expected to find their own lodgings and food. But the poor revolution had still a great deal of private misery to answer for, in the way of reduced wages. Those who live on the frivolities of mankind, or, what is the same thing, their luxuries, have two sets of victims to plunder – the consumer, and the real producer, or the operative. This is true where men are employed, but much truer in the case of females. The last are usually so helpless, that they often cling to oppression and wrong, rather than submit to be cast entirely upon the world. The *marchande de mode*[47] who employed Adrienne was as *rusée*[48] as a politician who had followed all the tergiversations of Gallic policy, since the year '89. She was fully aware of what a prize she possessed in the unpracticed girl, and she felt the importance of keeping her in ignorance of her own value. By paying the franc, it might give her assistant premature notions of her own importance; but, by bringing her down to fifteen sous, humility could be inculcated, and the chance of keeping her doubled. This, which would have defeated a bargain with any common *couturière*,[49] succeeded perfectly with Adrienne. She received her fifteen sous with humble thankfulness, in constant apprehension of losing even that miserable pittance. Nor would her employer consent to let her work by the piece, at which the dear child might have earned at least thirty sous, for she discovered that she had to deal with a person of conscience, and that in no mode could as much be possibly extracted from the assistant, as by confiding to her own honor. At nine each day she was to breakfast; at a quarter past nine, precisely, to commence work for her employer; at one, she had a remission of half an hour; and at six, she became her own mistress.

'I put confidence in you, mademoiselle,' said the *marchande de mode*, 'and leave you to yourself entirely. You will bring home the work as it is finished, and your money will be always ready. Should your grandmother occupy more of your time than common, on any occasion, you can make it up of yourself, by working a little earlier, or a little later; or, once in a while, you can throw in a day, to make up for lost time. You would not do as well at piecework, and I wish to deal generously by you. When certain things are wanted in a hurry, you will not mind working an hour or two beyond time, and I will always find lights with the greatest pleasure. Permit me to advise you to take the intermissions as much as possible for your attentions to your grandmother, who must be attended to properly. *Si* – the care of our parents is one of our most solemn duties! *Adieu, mademoiselle; au revoir!*'

This was one of the speeches of the *marchande de mode* to Adrienne, and the dear girl repeated it in her mind, as she sat at work on me, without the slightest distrust of the heartless selfishness it so ill concealed. On fifteen sous she found she could live without encroaching on the little stock set apart for the support of her grandmother, and she was content. Alas! The poor girl had not entered into any calculation of the expense of lodgings, of fuel, of clothes, of health impaired, and as for any resources for illness or accidents, she was totally without them. Still

Adrienne thought herself the obliged party, in times as critical as those which then hung over France, in being permitted to toil for a sum that would barely supply a grisette,[50] accustomed all her life to privations, with the coarsest necessaries.

I have little to say of the succeeding fortnight. Madame de la Rocheaimard gradually grew feebler, but she might still live months. No one could tell, and Adrienne hoped she would never die. Happily, her real wants were few, though her appetite was capricious, and her temper querulous. Love for her grandchild, however, shone in all she said and did, and so long as she was loved by this, the only being on earth she had ever been taught to love herself, Adrienne would not think an instant of the ills caused by the infirmities of age. She husbanded her money with the utmost frugality, and contrived to save even a few sous daily, out of her own wages, to add to her grandmother's stock. This she could not have done, but for the circumstance of there being so much in the house of their early stores, to help eke out the supplies of the moment. But, at the end of a fortnight, Adrienne found herself reduced to her last franc, including all her own savings. Something must be done, and that without delay, or Mme de la Rocheaimard would be without the means of support.

By this time Adrienne had little to dispose of, except the lace. This exquisite piece of human ingenuity had originally cost five louis d'or, and Adrienne had once shown it to her employer, who had generously offered to give two napoleons for it. But the lace must be kept for my gala dress, and it was hoped that it would bring at least its original cost when properly bestowed as an ornament on a fabric of my quality. There was the silver thimble, and that had cost five francs. Adrienne sent for the porter's daughter, and she went forth to dispose of this, almost the only article of luxury that remained to her.

'*Un dé, ma bonne demoiselle!*'[51] exclaimed the woman to whom the thimble was offered for sale; 'this is so common an article as scarcely to command any price. I will give thirty sous, notwithstanding.'

Adrienne had made her calculations, as she fancied, with some attention to the ways of the world. Bitter experience was teaching her severe lessons, and she felt the necessity of paying more attention than had been her wont to the practices of men. She had hoped to receive three francs for her thimble, which was quite new, and which, being pretty, was cheap at five, as sold in the shops. She ventured, therefore, to express as much to the woman in question.

'Three francs, mademoiselle!' exclaimed the other – '*Jamais*,[52] since the three days! All our commerce was then destroyed, and no one would think of giving such a price. If I get three for it myself I shall be too happy. *Cependant*,[53] as the thimble is pretty, and the metal looks good, we will say five and thirty sous, and have no more words about it.'

Adrienne sighed, and then she received the money and returned home. Two hours later the woman of the shop met with an idle customer who had more money than discretion, and she sold this very thimble for six francs, under the plea that it was a new fashion that had sprung out of the Revolution of July. That illustrious event, however, produced other results that were quite as hard to be reduced to the known connection between cause and effect as this.

Adrienne found that by using the wine that still remained, as well as some sugar and arrowroot, her grandmother could be made comfortable for just ten sous a day. She had been able to save of her own wages three, and here, then, were the means of maintaining Mme de la Rocheaimard, including the franc on hand, for just a week longer. To do this, however, some little extra economy would be necessary. Adrienne had conscientiously taken the time used to sell the thimble from her morning's work on me. As she sat down, on her return, she went over these calculations in her mind, and when they were ended, she cast a look at her work, as if to calculate its duration by what she had so far finished. Her eye assured her that not more than one fourth of her labor was, as yet, completed. Could she get over the next six weeks, however, she would be comparatively rich, and, as her lease would be out in two months, she determined to get cheaper lodgings in the country, remove her grandmother, purchase another handkerchief – if possible one of my family – and while she lived on the fruits of her present labors, to earn the means for a still more remote day. It is true, she had no more lace with which to decorate another handkerchief, but the sale of this would supply the money to purchase anew, and in this way the simple-minded girl saw no reason why she might not continue on as long as health and strength would allow – at least as long as her grandmother lived.

Hope is as blessed a provision for the poor and unhappy as occupation. While oppressed with present ills they struggle to obtain a fancied existence under happier auspices, furnishing a healthful and important lesson to man, that never ceases to remind him of a future that is to repair every wrong, apply a balm to every wound, if he will only make a timely provision for its wants.

Again did Adrienne resume her customary round of duties. Four hours each morning were devoted to me. Then followed the frugal breakfast, when her commoner toil for the milliner succeeded. The rest of the day was occupied with this latter work, for which she received the customary fifteen sous. When she retired at night, which the ailings and complaints of her grandmother seldom permitted before eleven, it was with a sense of weariness that began to destroy sleep; still the dear girl thought herself happy, for I more than equaled her expectations, and she had latterly worked on me with so much zeal as to have literally thrown the fruits of two weeks' work into one.

But the few francs Adrienne possessed diminished with alarming rapidity. She began to calculate her ways and means once more, and this was no longer done as readily as before. Her own wardrobe would not bear any drain upon it. Early in the indisposition of her grandmother, all of *that* had been sold that she could spare; for, with the disinterestedness of her nature, when sacrifices became necessary her first thoughts were of her own little stock of clothes. Of jewelry she never had been the mistress of much, though the vicomtesse had managed to save a few relics of her own ancient magnificence. Nevertheless, they were articles of but little value, the days of her exile having made many demands on all such resources.

It happened, one evening when Adrienne was receiving her wages from the milliner, that the poor girl overheard a discourse that proved she was not paid at the rate at which others were remunerated. Her eyes told her that her own work was the neatest in the shop, and she also saw that she did more than any other girl employed by the same person. As she knew her own expertness with the needle, this did not surprise her; but she felt some wonder that more and better work should produce the least reward. Little did she understand the artifices of the selfish and calculating, one of the most familiar of their frauds being to conceal from the skillful their own success, lest it should command a price in proportion to its claims. The milliner heard Adrienne's ladylike and gentle remonstrance with alarm, and she felt that she was in danger of losing a prize. But two expedients suggested themselves; to offer a higher price, or to undervalue the services she was so fearful of losing. Her practiced policy, as well as her selfishness, counseled her to try the latter expedient first.

'You amaze me, mademoiselle,' she answered, when Adrienne, trembling at her own resolution, ceased speaking. 'I was thinking myself whether I could afford to pay you fifteen sous, when so many young women who have been regularly brought up to the business are willing to work for less. I am afraid we must part, unless you can consent to receive twelve sous in future.'

Adrienne stood aghast. The very mirror of truth herself, she could not imagine that anyone – least of all any woman – could be so false and cruel as to practice the artifice to which the milliner had resorted; and, here, just as she saw a way opened by which she might support both her grandmother and herself until the handkerchief was completed, a change threatened her, by which she was to be left altogether without food. Still her conscience was so tender that she even doubted the propriety of accepting her old wages were she really incompetent to earn them.

'I had hoped, madame,' she said, the color coming and going on cheeks that were now usually pale – 'I had hoped, madame, that you found my work profitable. Surely, surely I bring home as much at night as any other demoiselle you employ.'

'In that there is not much difference, I allow, mademoiselle; but you can imagine that work done by one accustomed to the art is more likely to please customers than work done by one who has been educated as a lady. *Cependant*, I will not throw you off, as I know that your poor dear grandmother – '

'*Si – si*,' eagerly interrupted Adrienne, trembling from head to foot with apprehension.

'I know it all, mademoiselle, and the dear old lady shall not suffer; you shall both be made happy again on fifteen. To ease your mind, mademoiselle, I am willing to make a written contract for a year; at that rate, too, to put your heart at ease.'

'*Non – non – non*,' murmured Adrienne, happy and grateful for the moment, but unwilling to defeat her own plans for the future. 'Thank you, thank you, madame; tomorrow you shall see what I can do.'

And Adrienne toiled the succeeding day, not only until her fingers and body ached, but until her very heart ached. Poor child! Little did she think that she was establishing precedents against herself, by which further and destructive exertions might be required. But the apprehension of losing the pittance she actually received, and thereby blasting all hopes from me, was constantly before her mind, quickening her hand and sustaining her body.

During all this time Mme de la Rocheaimard continued slowly to sink. Old age, disappointments and poverty were working out their usual results, and death was near to close the scene. So gradual were the changes, however, that Adrienne did not note them, and accustomed as she had been to the existence, the presence, the love of this one being, and of this being only, to her the final separation scarce seemed within the bounds of possibility. Surely everything around the human family inculcates the doctrine of the mysterious future, and the necessity of living principally that they be prepared to die. All they produce perishes, all they imagine perishes, as does all they love. The union of two beings may be so engrossing, in their eyes, have lasted so long, and embraced so many ties, as to seem indissoluble; it is all seeming; the hour will infallibly come when the past becomes as nothing, except as it has opened the way to the future.

Adrienne at length, by dint of excessive toil, by working deep into the nights, by stinting herself of food, and by means of having disposed of the last article with which she could possibly part, had managed to support her grandmother and herself, until she saw me so far done as to be within another day's work of completion. At such a moment as this all feeling of vanity is out of the question. I was certainly very beautiful. A neater, a more tasteful, a finer, or a more exquisitely laced hand-kerchief, did not exist within the walls of Paris. In all that she figured to herself, as related to my appearance, the end justified her brightest expectations; but, as that end drew near, she felt how insufficient were human results to meet the desires of human hopes. Now that her painful and exhausting toil was nearly over, she did not experience the happiness she had anticipated. The fault was not in me, but in herself. Hope had exhausted her spirit, and as if merely to teach the vanity of the wishes of men, a near approach to the object that had seemed so desirable in the distance, had stripped off the mask and left the real countenance exposed. There was nothing unusual in this; it was merely following out a known law of nature.

7

The morning of the 14th June arrived. Paris is then at its loveliest season. The gardens in particular are worthy of the capital of Europe, and they are open to all who can manage to make a decent appearance. Adrienne's hotel had a little garden in the rear, and she sat at her window endeavoring to breathe the balmy odors that arose from it. Enter it she could not. It was the property, or devoted to the uses, of the occupant of the *rez de chaussée*[54]. Still she might look at it as often as she dared to raise her eyes from her needle. The poor girl was not what she had been two months before. The handkerchief wanted but a few hours of being finished, it is true, but the pale cheeks, the hollow eyes and the anxious look proved at what a sacrifice of health and physical force I had become what I was. As I had grown in beauty, the hand that ornamented me had wasted, and when I looked up to catch the smile of approbation, it was found to be careworn and melancholy. Still the birds did not sing the less sweetly, for Paris is full of birds, the roses were as fragrant, and the verdure was as deep as ever. Nature does not stop to lament over any single victim of human society. When misery is the deepest, there is something awful in this perpetual and smiling round of natural movements. It teaches profoundly the insignificance of the atoms of creation.

Adrienne had risen earlier than common, even, this morning, determined to get through with her task by noon, for she was actually sewing on the lace, and her impatience would not permit her to resume the work of the milliner that day, at least. For the last month she had literally lived on dry bread herself, at first with a few grapes to give her appetite a little gratification, but toward the last, on nothing but bread and water. She had not suffered so much from a want of food, however, as from a want of air and exercise, from unremitting, wasting toil at a sedentary occupation, from hope deferred and from sleepless nights. Then she wanted the cheering association of sympathy. She was strictly alone; with the exception of her short interviews with the milliner, she conversed with no one. Her grandmother slept most of the time, and when she did speak, it was with the querulousness of disease, and not in the tones of affection. This was hardest of all to bear; but Adrienne did bear up under all, flattering herself that when she could remove Mme de la Rocheaimard into the country, her grandmother would revive and become as fond of her as ever. She toiled on, therefore, though she could not altogether suppress her tears. Under her painful and pressing circumstances, the poor girl felt her deepest affliction to be that she had not time to pray. Her work, now that she had nothing to expect from the milliner, could not be laid aside for a moment, though her soul did pour out its longings as she sat plying her needle.

Fortunately, Mme de la Rocheaimard was easy and tranquil the whole of the last morning. Although nearly exhausted by her toil and the want of food, for Adrienne had eaten her last morsel, half a roll, at breakfast, she continued to toil; but the work was nearly done, and the dear girl's needle fairly flew. Of a sudden she dropped me in her lap and burst into a flood of tears. Her sobs were hysterical, and I felt afraid she would faint. A glass of water, however, restored her, and then this outpouring of an exhausted nature was suppressed. I was completed! At that instant, if not the richest, I was probably the neatest and most tasteful handkerchief in Paris. At this critical moment, Desirée, the *commissionaire*, entered the room.

From the moment that Adrienne had purchased me, this artful woman had never lost sight of the intended victim. By means of an occasional bribe to little Nathalie, she ascertained the precise progress of the work, and learning that I should probably be ready for sale that very morning, under the pretence of hiring the apartment, she was shown into my important presence. A brief apology explained all, and Adrienne civilly showed her little rooms.

'When does your lease end, mademoiselle?' demanded Desirée, carelessly.

'Next week, madame. I intend to remove to the country with my grandmother the beginning of the week.'

'You will do very right; no one that has the means should stay in Paris after June. *Dieu!* What a beautiful handkerchief! Surely – surely – this is not your work, mademoiselle?'

Adrienne simply answered in the affirmative, and then the *commissionaire's* admiration was redoubled. Glancing her eye round the room, as if to ascertain the probabilities, the woman inquired if the handkerchief was ordered. Adrienne blushed, but shaking off the transient feeling of shame, she stated that it was for sale.

'I know a lady who would buy this – a *marchande de mode*, a friend of mine, who gives the highest prices that are ever paid for such articles – for to tell you the truth certain Russian princesses employ her in all these little matters. Have you thought of your price, mademoiselle?'

Adrienne's bloom had actually returned, with this unexpected gleam of hope, for the affair of disposing of me had always appeared awful in her imagination. She owned the truth frankly, and said that she had not made herself acquainted with the prices of such things, except as she had understood what affluent ladies paid for them.

'Ah! that is a different matter,' said Desirée, coldly. 'These ladies pay far more than a thing is worth. Now you paid ten francs for the handkerchief itself.'

'Twenty-eight,' answered Adrienne, trembling.

'Twenty-eight! mademoiselle, they deceived you shamefully. Ten would have been dear in the present absence of strangers from Paris. No, call *that* ten. This lace would probably bring a napoleon – yes, I think it might bring a napoleon.'

Adrienne's heart sunk within her. She had supposed it to be worth at least five times as much.

'That makes thirty francs,' continued Desirée coldly; 'and now for the work. You must have been a fortnight doing all this pretty work.'

'Two months, madame,' said Adrienne, faintly.

'Two months! Ah! you are not accustomed to this sort of work and are not adroit, perhaps.'

'I worked only in the mornings and late at night; but still think I worked full hours.'

'Yes, you worked when sleepy. Call it a month, then. Thirty days at ten sous a day make fifteen francs. Ten for the handkerchief, twenty for the lace, and fifteen for the work, make forty-five francs – *parole d'honneur*,[55] it does come to a pretty price for a handkerchief. *Si*, we must ask forty-five francs for it, and then we can always abate the five francs, and take two napoleons.'

Adrienne felt sick at heart. Want of nourishment had lessened her energies, and here came a blow to all her golden visions that was near overcoming her. She knew that handkerchiefs similar to this frequently sold for twenty napoleons in the shops, but she did not know how much the cupidity of trade extracted from the silly and vain in the way of sheer contributions to avarice. It is probable the unfortunate young lady would have lost her consciousness, under the weight of this blow, had it not been for the sound of her grandmother's feeble voice calling her to the bedside. This was a summons that Adrienne never disregarded, and, for the moment, she forgot her causes of grief.

'My poor Adrienne,' whispered Mme de la Rocheaimard in a tone of tenderness that her granddaughter had not heard for some weeks, 'my poor Adrienne, the hour is near when we must part – '

'Grandmamma! – dearest grandmamma!'

'Nay, love, God wills it. I am old, and I feel death upon me. It is happy that he comes so gently, and when I am so well prepared to meet him. The grave has views, that no other scene offers, Adrienne! Noble blood and ancient renown are as nothing compared to God's mercy and forgiveness. Pardon me if I have ever taught thy simple heart to dwell on vanities; but it was a fault of the age. This world is all vanity, and I can now see it when it is too late. Do not let *my* fault be *thy* fault, child of my love. Kiss me, Adrienne, pray for my soul when all is over.'

'Yes, dearest, dearest grandmamma, thou know'st I will.'

'Thou must part with the rest of the trousseau to make thyself comfortable when I am gone.'

'I will do as thou wishest, dearest grandmamma.'

'Perhaps it will raise enough to purchase thee four or five hundred francs of *rentes*,[56] on which thou may'st live with frugality.'

'Perhaps it will, grandmamma.'

'Thou wilt not sell the thimble – *that* thou wilt keep to remember me.'

43

Adrienne bowed her head and groaned. Then her grandmother desired her to send for a priest, and her thoughts took another direction. It was fortunate they did, for the spirit of the girl could not have endured more.

That night Mme de la Rocheaimard died, the wife of the porter, the *bon curé*, and Adrienne alone being present. Her last words were a benediction on the fair and gentle being who had so faithfully and tenderly nursed her in old age. When all was over, and the body was laid out, Adrienne asked to be left alone with it. Living or dead, her grandmother could never be an object of dread to her, and there were few disposed to watch. In the course of the night, Adrienne even caught a little sleep, a tribute that nature imperiously demanded of her weakness.

The following day was one of anguish and embarrassment. The physician, who always inspects the dead in France, came to make his report. The arrangements were to be ordered for the funeral. Fortunately, as Adrienne then thought, Desirée appeared in the course of the morning, as one who came in consequence of having been present at so much of the scene of the preceding day. In her character of a *commissionaire* she offered her services, and Adrienne, unaccustomed to act for herself in such offices, was fain to accept them. She received an order, or rather an answer to a suggestion of her own, and hurried off to give the necessary directions. Adrienne was now left alone again with the body of her deceased grandmother. As soon as the excitement ceased, she began to feel languid, and she became sensible of her own bodily wants. Food of no sort had passed her lips in more than thirty hours, and her last meal had been a scanty breakfast of dry bread. As the faintness of hunger came over her, Adrienne felt for her purse with the intention of sending Nathalie to a neighboring baker's, when the truth flashed upon her, in its dreadful reality. She had not a *liard*[57]. Her last sou had furnished the breakfast of the preceding day. A sickness like that of death came over her, when, casting her eyes around her in despair, they fell on the little table that usually held the nourishment prepared for her grandmother. A little arrowroot, and a light potage, which contained bread, still remained. Although it was all that seemed to separate the girl from death, she hesitated about using it. There was

44

an appearance of sacrilege, in her eyes, in the act of appropriating these things to herself. A moment's reflection, however, brought her to a truer state of mind, and then she felt it to be a duty to that dear parent herself, to renew her own strength, in order to discharge her duty to the dead. She ate, therefore, though it was with a species of holy reverence. Her strength was renewed, and she was enabled to relieve her soul by prayer.

'Mademoiselle will have the goodness to give me ten francs,' said Desirée, on her return; 'I have ordered every thing that is proper, but money is wanting to pay for some little articles that will soon come.'

'I have no money, Desirée – not even a sou.'

'No money, mademoiselle? In the name of heaven, how are we to bury your grandmother?'

'The handkerchief – '

Desirée shook her head, and saw that she must countermand most of the orders. Still she was human, and she was a female. She could not altogether desert one so helpless, in a moment of such extreme distress. She reflected on the matter for a minute or two, and opened her mind.

'This handkerchief might sell for forty-five francs, mademoiselle,' she said, 'and I will pay that much for it myself, and will charge nothing for my services today. Your dear grandmother must have Christian burial, that is certain, and poor enough will that be which is had for two napoleons. What say you, mademoiselle – will you accept the forty-five francs, or would you prefer seeing the *marchande de mode?*'

'I can see no one now, Desirée. Give me the money, and do honor to the remains of my dear, dear grandmother.'

Adrienne said this with her hands resting on her lap in quiescent despair. Her eyes were hollow and vacant, her cheeks bloodless, her mind almost as helpless as that of an infant. Desirée laid down two napoleons, keeping the five francs to pay for some necessaries, and then she took me in her hands, as if to ascertain whether she had done too much. Satisfied on this head, I was carefully replaced in the basket, when the *commissionaire* went out again, on her errands, honorably disposed to be useful. Still she did not deem it necessary to conceal her employer's poverty, which was soon divulged to the porteress, and by her to the bourgeois.

Adrienne had now the means of purchasing food, but, ignorant how much might be demanded on behalf of the approaching ceremony, she religiously adhered to the use of dry bread. When Desirée returned in the evening, she told the poor girl that the *convoi*[58] was arranged for the following morning, that she had ordered all in the most economical way, but that thirty-five francs were the lowest sou for which the funeral could be had. Adrienne counted out the money, and then found herself the mistress of just four francs ten sous. When Desirée took her leave for the night, she placed me in her basket, and carried me to her own lodgings, in virtue of her purchase.

I was laid upon a table where I could look through an open window, up at the void of heaven. It was glittering with those bright stars that the astronomers tell us are suns of other systems, and the scene gradually drew me to reflections on that eternity that is before us. My feelings got to be gradually soothed, as I remembered the moment of time that all are required to endure injustice and wrongs on earth. Some such reflections are necessary to induce us to submit to the mysterious reign of Providence, whose decrees so often seem unequal, and whose designs are so inscrutable. By remembering what a speck is time, as compared with eternity, and that 'God chasteneth those he loveth,'[59] the ills of life may be borne, even with joy.

The manner in which Desirée disposed of me, shall be related in another number.[60]

8

The reader is not to infer that Desirée was unusually mercenary. That she was a little addicted to this weakness is true – who ever knew a *commissionaire* that was not? But she had her moments of benevolence, as well as others, and had really made some sacrifice of her time, and consequently of her interests, in order to serve Adrienne in her distress. As for the purchase of myself, that was in the way of her commerce; and it is seldom, indeed, that philanthropy can overcome the habits of trade.

Desirée was not wholly without means, and she was in no hurry to reap the benefit of her purchase. I remained in her possession, according to my calculation, some two or three years before she ever took me out of the drawer in which I had been deposited for safe keeping. I was considered a species of *corps de reserve*.[61] At the end of that period, however, her thoughts recurred to her treasure, and an occasion soon offered for turning me to account. I was put into the reticule, and carried about, in readiness for any suitable bargain that might turn up.

One day Desirée and I were on the Boulevards Italiens together, when a figure caught the *commissionaire*'s eye that sent her across the street in a great hurry. I scarcely know how to describe this person, who, to my simple eyes, had the appearance of a colonel of the late Royal Guards, or, at least, of an attaché of one of the northern legations. He was dressed in the height of the latest fashion, as well as he knew how to be, wore terrible moustaches, and had a rare provision of rings, eyeglasses, watch guards, chains, &c.

'*Bonjour, monsieur,*' exclaimed Desirée, in haste, '*parole d'honneur*, I scarcely knew you! I have been waiting for your return from Lyons with the most lively impatience, for, to tell you the truth, I have the greatest bijou for your American ladies that ever came out of a bleaching ground – *un mouchoir de poche*.'[62]

'*Doucement*[63] – *doucement, ma bonne,*' interrupted the other, observing that the woman was about to exhibit me on the open Boulevards, an exposé for which he had no longings, 'you can bring it to my lodgings – '

'Rue de Clery, *numéro cent vingt* – '[64]

'Not at all, my good Desirée. You must know I have transacted all my ordinary business – made my purchases, and am off for New York in the next packet – '

'*Mais, le malle,*[65] *monsieur?*'

'Yes, the trunk will have a corner in it for anything particular, as you say. I shall go to court this evening, to a great ball, Madame la Marquise de Dolomien and the Aide de Camp de Service having just notified me that I am invited. To be frank with you, Desirée, I am lodging in la Rue de la Paix, and appear, just now, as a mere traveler. You will inquire for *le Colonel Silky*, when you call.'

'*Le Colonel Silky!*' repeated Desirée with a look of admiration, a little mingled with contempt.

'*De la garde nationale Américaine*,'[66] answered Mr. Silky, smiling. He then gave the woman his new address, and appointed an hour to see her.

Desirée was punctual to a minute. The porter, the *garçons*,[67] the bourgeois, all knew le Colonel Silky, who was now a great man, wore moustaches, and went to court – as the court was. In a minute the *commissionaire* was in the colonel's antechamber. This distinguished officer had a method in his madness. He was not accustomed to keeping a body servant, and, as his aim was to make a fortune, will ye nill ye, he managed, even now, in his hours of pride and self-indulgence, to get along without one. It was not many moments, therefore, before he came out and ushered Desirée himself into his *salon*,[68] a room of ten feet by fourteen, with a carpet that covered just eight feet by six, in its centre. Now that they were alone, in this snuggery, which seemed barely large enough to contain so great a man's moustaches, the parties understood each other without unnecessary phrases, and I was, at once, produced.

Colonel Silky was evidently struck with my appearance. An officer of his readiness and practice saw at once that I might be made to diminish no small part of the ways and means of his present campaign, and precisely in proportion as he admired me, he began to look cold and indifferent. This management could not deceive me, my clairvoyance defying any such artifices; but it had a sensible effect on Desirée, who, happening very much to want money for a particular object just at that moment, determined, on the spot, to abate no less than fifty francs from the price she had intended to ask. This was deducting five francs more than poor Adrienne got for the money she had expended for her beautiful lace, and for all her toil, sleepless nights, and tears, a proof of the *commissionaire*'s scale of doing business. The bargain was now commenced in earnest, offering an instructive scene of French protestations, assertions, contradictions and volubility on one side, and of cold, seemingly phlegmatic, but wily Yankee calculation, on the other. Desirée had set her price at 150 francs, after abating the fifty mentioned, and Colonel Silky had early made up his mind to give only 100. After making suitable allowances for my true value before I was embellished, the cost of the lace and of the work, Desirée was not far from the mark; but the Colonel saw that she wanted money, and he knew that two napoleons and a half, with his management, would carry him from Paris to Havre. It is true he had spent the difference that morning on an eyeglass that he never used, or when he did it was only to obscure his vision; but the money was not lost, as it aided in persuading the world he was a colonel and was afflicted with that genteel defect, an imperfect vision. These extremes of extravagance and meanness were not unusual in his practice. The one, in truth, being a consequence of the other.

'You forget the duty, Desirée,' observed the military trader; 'this compromise law[69] is a thousand times worse than any law we have ever had in America.'

'The duty!' repeated the woman, with an incredulous smile; 'monsieur, you are not so young as to pay any duty on a pocket hand-kerchief! *Ma foi*, I will bring twenty – *oui*, a thousand from England itself, and the *douaniers*[70] shall not stop one.'

'Aye, but we don't smuggle in America,' returned the colonel, with an aplomb that might have done credit to Vidocq[71] himself; 'in our republican country the laws are all in all.'

'Why do so many of your good republicans dress so that the rue de Clery don't know them, and then go to the château?' demanded the *commissionaire*, very innocently, as to appearance at least.

'Bah! there are the five napoleons – if you want them, take them – if not, I care little about it, my invoice being all closed.'

Desirée never accepted money more reluctantly. Instead of making 155 francs out of the toil and privations and self-denial of poor Adrienne, she found her own advantages unexpectedly lessened to fifty-five, or, only a trifle more than 100 percent. But the colonel was firm, and, for once, her cupidity was compelled to succumb. The money was paid, and I became the vassal of Colonel Silky, a titular soldier, but a traveling trader, who never lost sight of the main chance either in his campaigns, his journeys, or his pleasures.

To own the truth, Colonel Silky was delighted with me. No girl could be a better judge of the *article*, and all his cultivated taste ran into the admiration of goods. I was examined with the closest scrutiny; my merits were inwardly applauded, and my demerits pronounced to be absolutely none. In short, I was flattered; for, it must be confessed, the commendation of even a fool is grateful. So far from placing me in a trunk, or a drawer, the colonel actually put me in his pocket, though duly enveloped and with great care, and for some time I trembled in every delicate fiber, lest, in a moment of forgetfulness, he might use me. But my new master had no such intention. His object in taking me out was to consult a sort of court *commissionaire*, with whom he had established certain relations, and that, too, at some little cost, on the propriety of using me himself that evening at the château of the King of the French. Fortunately, his monitress, though by no means of the purest water, knew better than to suffer her *élève*[72] to commit so gross a blunder, and I escaped the calamity of making my first appearance at court under the auspices of such a patron.

There was a moment, too, when the colonel thought of presenting me to Mme de Dolomien, by the way of assuring his favor in the royal circle, but when he came to count up the money he should lose in the way of profits, this idea became painful, and it was abandoned. As often happened with this gentleman, he reasoned so long in all his acts of liberality that he supposed a sufficient sacrifice had been made in the mental discussions, and he never got beyond what surgeons call the 'first intention' of his moral cures. The evening he went to court, therefore, I was carefully consigned to a *carton*[73] in the colonel's trunk, whence I did not again issue until my arrival in America. Of the voyage, therefore, I have little to say, not having had a sight of the ocean at all. I cannot affirm that I was absolutely seasick, but, on the other hand, I cannot add that I was perfectly well during any part of the passage. The pent air of the stateroom, and a certain heaviness about the brain, quite incapacitated me from enjoying anything that passed, and that was a happy moment when our trunk was taken on deck to be examined. The custom-house officers at New York were not men likely to pick out a pocket handkerchief from a gentleman's – I beg pardon, from a colonel's – wardrobe, and I passed unnoticed among sundry other of my employer's speculations. I call the colonel my *employer*, though this was not strictly true; for, Heaven be praised! he never did employ me; but ever since my arrival in America, my gorge has so risen against the word 'master' that I cannot make up my mind to write it. I know there is an ingenious substitute, as the following little dialogue will show, but my early education under the astronomer and the delicate-minded Adrienne has rendered me averse to false taste, and I find the substitute as disagreeable as the original. The conversation to which I allude, occurred between me and a very respectable looking shirt, that I happened to be hanging next to on a line, a few days after my arrival, the colonel having judged it prudent to get me washed and properly ironed, before he carried me into the 'market.'

'Who is your *boss*, pocket handkerchief?' demanded the shirt, a perfect stranger to me, by the way, for I had never seen him before the accidents of the washtub brought us in collision; 'who is your boss, pocket handkerchief, I say? – you are so very fine, I should like to know something of your history.'

From all I had heard and read, I was satisfied my neighbor was a Yankee shirt, both from his curiosity and from his abrupt manner of asking questions; still I was at a loss to know the meaning of the word *boss*, my clairvoyance being totally at fault. It belongs to no language known to the savans[74] or academicians.

'I am not certain, sir,' I answered, 'that I understand your meaning. What is a *boss*?'

'Oh! that's only a republican word for "master." Now, Judge Latitat is *my* boss, and a very good one he is, with the exception of his sitting so late at night at his infernal circuits, by the light of miserable tallow candles. But all the judges are alike for that, keeping a poor shirt up sometimes until midnight, listening to cursed dull lawyers, and prosy, caviling witnesses.'

'I beg you to recollect, sir, that I am a female pocket handkerchief, and persons of your sex are bound to use temperate and proper language in the presence of ladies.'

'Yes, I see you are feminine, by your ornaments – still, you might tell a fellow who is your boss?'

'I belong, at present, to Colonel Silky, if that is what you mean; but I presume some fair lady will soon do me the honor of transferring me to her own wardrobe. No doubt my future employer – is not that the word? – will be one of the most beautiful and distinguished ladies of New York.'

'No question of that, as money makes both beauty and distinction in this part of the world, and it's not a dollar that will buy you. *Colonel* Silky? I don't remember the name – which of *our* editors is he?'

'I don't think he is an editor at all. At least, I never heard he was employed about any publication, and, to own the truth, he does not appear to me to be particularly qualified for such a duty, either by native capacity, or, its substitute, education.'

'Oh! that makes no great difference – half the corps is exactly in the same predicament. I'fegs![75] if we waited for colonels, or editors either, in this country, until we got such as were qualified, we should get no news, and be altogether without politics, and the militia would soon be in an awful state.'

'This is very extraordinary! So you do not wait, but take them as they come. And what state is your militia actually in?'

'Awful! It is what my boss, the judge, sometimes calls a "statu quo."'

'And the newspapers – and the news – and the politics?'

'Why, they are *not* in "statu quo" – but in a "*semper eadem*"[76] – I beg pardon, do you understand Latin?'

'No, sir – ladies do not often study the dead languages.'

'If they did they would soon bring 'em to life! "*Semper eadem*" is Latin for "worse and worse." The militia is drilling into a "statu quo," and the press is enlightening mankind with a "*semper eadem*."'

After properly thanking my neighbor for these useful explanations, we naturally fell into discourse about matters and things in general, the weather in America being uniformly too fine to admit of discussion.

'Pray, sir,' said I, trembling lest my *boss* might be a colonel of the editorial corps, after all – 'pray, sir,' said I, 'is it expected in this country that the wardrobe should entertain the political sentiments of its boss?'

'I rather think not, unless it might be in high party times; or, in the case of editors, and such extreme patriots. I have several relatives that belong to the corps, and they all tell me that while their bosses very frequently change their coats, they are by no means so particular about changing their shirts. But you are of foreign birth, ma'am, I should think by your dress and appearance?'

'Yes, sir, I came quite recently from France; though, my employer being American, I suppose I am entitled to the rights of citizenship. Are you European, also?'

'No, ma'am; I am native and to the "*manor* born," as the modern Shakespeare has it.[77] Is Louis Philippe likely to maintain the throne, in France?'

'That is not so certain, sir, by what I learn, as that the throne is likely to maintain Louis Philippe. To own the truth to you, I am a Carlist,[78] as all genteel articles are, and I enter but little into the subject of Louis Philippe's reign.'

This remark made me melancholy, by reviving the recollection of Adrienne, and the conversation ceased. An hour or two later, I was removed from the line, properly ironed, and returned to my boss. The same day I was placed in a shop in Broadway, belonging to a firm of which I now understood the colonel was a sleeping partner. A suitable entry was made against me, in a private memorandum book, which, as I once had an opportunity of seeing it, I will give here.

> *Super-extraordinary Pocket handkerchief, French cambric, trimmed and worked, in account with Bobbinet & Gull.*
> DR.
> To money paid first cost, francs 100, at 5.25 – $19.04
> To interest on same for – 00.00
> To portion of passage money – 00.04
> To porterage – 00.00 1/4
> To washing and making up – 00.25
> (*Mem.* – See if a deduction cannot be made from this charge.)
> CR.
> By cash, for allowing Miss Thimble to copy pattern – not to be worked until our article is sold – $1.00
> By cash for sale, &c. –

Thus the account stood the day I was first offered to the admiration of the fair of New York. Mr. Bobbinet, however, was in no hurry to exhibit me, having several articles of less beauty, that he was anxious to get off first. For my part, I was as desirous of being produced, as ever a young lady was to come out; and then my companions in the drawer were not of the most agreeable character. We were all pocket handkerchiefs, together, and all of French birth. Of the whole party, I was the only one that had been worked by a real lady, and consequently my education was manifestly superior to those of my companions. *They* could scarcely be called comme il faut, at all; though, to own the truth, I am afraid there is *tant soit peu de*[79] vulgarity about all *worked* pocket handkerchiefs. I remember that, one day, when Mme de la Rocheaimard and Adrienne were discussing the expediency of buying our whole piece, with a view of offering us to their benefactress, the former, who had a fine tact in matters of this sort, expressed a doubt whether the dauphine would be pleased with such an offering.

'Her Royal Highness, like all cultivated minds, looks for fitness in her ornaments and tastes. What fitness is there, *ma chère*,[80] in converting an article of real use, and which should not be paraded to one's associates, into an article of senseless luxury? I know there are two doctrines on this important point – '

But, as I shall have occasion, soon, to go into the whole philosophy of this matter, when I come to relate the manner of my next purchase, I will not stop here to relate all that Mme de la Rocheaimard said. It is sufficient that she, a woman of tact in such matters at least, had strong doubts concerning the *taste* and propriety of using worked pocket handkerchiefs, at all.

My principal objection to my companions in the drawer was their incessant senseless repinings about France, and their abuse of the country in which they were to pass their lives. I could see enough in America to find fault with, through the cracks of the drawer, and if an American, I might have indulged a little in the same way myself, for I am not one of those who think fault-finding belongs properly to the stranger, and not to the native. It is the proper office of the latter, as it is his duty to amend these faults, the traveler being bound in justice to look at the good as well as the evil. But, according to my companions, there was *nothing* good in America – the climate, the people, the food, the morals, the laws, the dress, the manners, and the tastes, were all infinitely worse than those they had been accustomed to. Even the physical proportions of the population were condemned, without mercy. I confess I was surprised at hearing the *size* of the Americans sneered at by *pocket handkerchiefs*, as I remember to have read that the *noses* of the New Yorkers, in particular, were materially larger than common. When the supercilious and vapid point out faults, they ever run into contradictions and folly; it is only under the lash of the discerning and the experienced that we betray by our writhings the power of the blow we receive.

9

I might have been a fortnight in the shop, when I heard a voice as gentle and ladylike as that of Adrienne, inquiring for pocket hand-kerchiefs. My heart fairly beat for joy; for, to own the truth, I was getting to be wearied to death with the garrulous folly of my com-panions. They had so much of the *couturières* about them! not one of the whole party ever having been a regular employee in genteel life. Their *niaiseries*[81] were endless, and there was just as much of the low-bred anticipation as to their future purchases, as one sees at the balls of the *Champs Elysées* on the subject of partners. The word 'pocket handkerchief,' and that so sweetly pronounced, drew open our drawer, as it might be, instinctively. Two or three dozen of us, all of exquisite fineness, were laid upon the counter, myself and two or three more of the better class being kept a little in the background, as a skillful general holds his best troops in reserve.

The customers were sisters; that was visible at a glance. Both were pretty, almost beautiful – and there was an air of simplicity about their dress, a quiet and unobtrusive dignity in their manners, which at once announced them to be real ladies. Even the tones of their voices were polished, a circumstance that I think one is a little apt to notice in New York. I discovered, in the course of the conversation, that they were the daughters of a gentleman of very large estate, and belonged to the true elite of the country. The manner in which the clerks received them, indeed, proclaimed this; for, though their other claims might not have so promptly extracted this homage, their known wealth would.

Mr. Bobbinet attended these customers in person. Practiced in all that portion of human knowledge that appertains to a salesman, he let the sweet girls select two or three dozen handkerchiefs of great beauty, but totally without ornament, and even pay for them, before he said a word on the subject of the claims of his reserved corps. When he thought the proper moment had arrived, however, one of the least decorated of our party was offered to the consideration of the young ladies. The sisters were named Anne and Maria, and I could see by the pleasure that beamed in the soft blue eyes of the former that she was quite enchanted with the beauty of the *article* laid before her so unexpectedly. I believe it is in *female* 'human nature' to admire every thing that is graceful and handsome, and especially when it takes the form of needlework. The sweet girls praised handkerchief after handkerchief, until I was laid before them, when their pleasure extracted exclamations of delight. All was done so quietly, however, and in so ladylike a manner, that the attention of no person in the shop was drawn to them by this natural indulgence of surprise. Still I observed that neither of the young lades inquired the *prices*, these being considerations that had no influence on the intrinsic value, in their eyes; while the circumstance caused my heart to sink within me, as it clearly proved they did not intend to purchase, and I longed to become the property of the gentle, serene-eyed Anne. After thanking Mr. Bobbinet for the trouble he had taken, they ordered their purchases sent home, and were about to quit the shop.

'Can't I persuade you to take *this*?' demanded Bobbinet, as they were turning away. 'There is not its equal in America. Indeed, one of the house, our Colonel Silky, who has just returned from Paris, says it was worked expressly for the dauphine, who was prevented from getting it by the late revolution.'

'It *is* a pity so much lace and such exquisite work should be put on a pocket handkerchief,' said Anne, almost involuntarily. 'I fear if they were on something more suitable, I might buy them.'

A smile, a slight blush, and curtsy, concluded the interview; and the young ladies hastily left the shop. Mr. Bobbinet was disappointed, as, indeed, was Col. Silky, who was present, *en amateur*;[82] but the matter could not be helped, as these were customers who acted and thought for themselves, and all the oily persuasion of shop-eloquence could not influence them.

'It is quite surprising, colonel,' observed Mr. Bobbinet, when his customers were properly out of hearing, 'that *these* young ladies should let such an article slip through their fingers. Their father is one of the richest men we have; and yet they never even asked the price.'

'I fancy it was not so much the *price* that held 'em back,' observed the colonel, in his elegant way, 'as something else. There are a sort of customers that don't buy promiscuously; they do every thing by rule. They don't believe that a nightcap is intended for a bed-quilt.'

Bobbinet & Co. did not exactly understand his more sophisticated partner; but before he had time to ask an explanation, the appearance of another customer caused his face to brighten, and changed the current of his thoughts. The person who now entered was an exceedingly brilliant looking girl of twenty, dressed in the height of fashion, and extremely well, though a severe critic might have thought she was *over* dressed for the streets; still she had alighted from a carriage. Her face was decidedly handsome, and her person exquisitely proportioned. As a whole, I had scarcely ever seen a young creature that could lay claim to more of the loveliness of her sex. Both the young ladies who had just left us were pleasing and pretty; and to own the truth, there was an air of modest refinement about them, that was not so apparent in this new visitor; but the dazzling appearance of the latter, at first, blinded me to her faults, and I saw nothing but her perfection. The interest manifested by the master – I beg his pardon, the boss of the store – and the agitation among the clerks, very plainly proved that much was expected from the visit of this young lady, who was addressed, with a certain air of shop-familiarity, as Miss Halfacre – a familiarity that showed she was an habitué of the place, and considered a good customer.

Luckily for the views of Bobbinet & Co., we were all still lying on the counter. This is deemed a fortunate circumstance in the contingencies of this species of trade, since it enables the dealer to offer his uncalled-for wares in the least suspicious and most natural manner. It was fortunate, also, that I lay at the bottom of the little pile – a climax being quite as essential in sustaining an extortionate price, as in terminating with due effect, a poem, a tragedy, or a romance.

'Good morning, Miss Halfacre,' said Mr. Bobbinet, bowing and smiling; if his face had been half as honest as it professed to be, it would have *grinned*. 'I am glad you have come in at this moment, as we are about to put on sale some of the rarest articles, in the way of pocket handkerchiefs, that have ever come to this market. The Misses Burton have just seen them, and *they* pronounce them the most beautiful articles of the sort they have ever seen; and I believe they have been over half the world.'

'And did they take any, Mr. Bobbinet? The Miss Burtons are thought to have taste.'

'They have not exactly *purchased*, but I believe each of them has a particular article in her eye. Here is one, ma'am, that is rather prettier than any you have yet seen in New York. The price is *sixty* dollars.'

The word *sixty* was emphasized in a way to show the importance that was attached to *price* – that being a test of more than common importance with the present customer. I sighed when I remembered that poor Adrienne had received but about ten dollars for *me* – an article worth so much more than that there exhibited.

'It is really very pretty, Mr. Bobbinet, very pretty, but Miss Monson bought one not quite as pretty, at Lace's; and *she* paid *sixty-five*, if I am not mistaken.'

'I dare say; we have them at much higher prices. I showed you *this* only that you might see that *our sixties* are as handsome as *Mr. Lace's* sixty-*fives*. What do you think of *this*?'

'That *is* a jewel! What *is* the price, Mr. Bobbinet?'

'Why, we will let *you* have it for seventy, though I do think it ought to bring five more.'

'Surely you do not abate on pocket handkerchiefs! One doesn't like to have such a thing *too* low.'

'Ah, I may as well come to the point at once with such a customer as yourself, Miss Halfacre; here is the article on which I pride myself. *That* article never *was* equaled in this market, and never *will* be.'

I cannot repeat half the exclamations of delight that escaped the fair Eudosia, when I first burst on her entranced eye. She turned me over and over, examined me with palpitating bosom, and once I thought she was about to kiss me; then, in a trembling voice, she demanded the price.

'*One hundred dollars*, ma'am;' answered Bobbinet, solemnly. 'Not a cent more, on my honor.'

'No, surely!' exclaimed Eudosia, with delight instead of alarm. 'Not a *hundred*!'

'*One hundred*, Miss Eudosia, to the last cent; then we scarcely make a living profit.'

'Why, Mr. Bobbinet, this is the highest-priced handkerchief that was ever sold in New York.' This was said with a sort of rapture, the fair creature feeling all the advantage of having so good an opportunity of purchasing so dear an *article*.

'In America, ma'am. It is the highest-priced handkerchief, by twenty dollars, that ever crossed the Atlantic. The celebrated Miss Jewel's, of Boston, only cost seventy-nine.'

'Only! Oh, Mr. Bobbinet, I *must* have it. It is a perfect treasure!'

'Shall I send it, Miss Eudosia; or don't you like to trust it out of your sight?'

'Not yet, sir. To own the truth, I have not so much money. I only came out to buy a few trifles, and brought but fifty dollars with me; and Pa insists on having no bills. I never knew anybody as particular as Pa; but I will go instantly home and show him the importance of this purchase. You will not let the handkerchief be seen for *one* hour – only *one* hour – and then you shall hear from me.'

To this Bobbinet assented. The young lady tripped into her carriage, and was instantly whirled from the door. In precisely forty-three minutes, a maid entered, half out of breath, and laid a note on the counter. The latter contained Mr. Halfacre's check for one hundred dollars, and a request from the fair Eudosia that I might be delivered to her messenger. Every thing was done as she had desired, and, in five minutes, I was going up Broadway as fast as Honor O'Flagherty's (for such was the name of the messenger) little dumpy legs could carry me.

10

Mr. Henry Halfacre was a speculator in town-lots – a profession that was, just then, in high repute in the city of New York. For farms, and all the more vulgar aspects of real estate, he had a sovereign contempt; but offer him a bit of land that could be measured by feet and inches, and he was your man. Mr. Halfacre inherited nothing, but he was a man of what are called energy and enterprise. In other words, he had a spirit for running in debt, and never shrunk from jeoparding property that, in truth, belonged to his creditors. The very morning that his eldest child, Eudosia, made her valuable acquisition, in my person, Henry Halfacre, Esq., was the owner of several hundred lots on the island of Manhattan; of 123 in the city of Brooklyn; of nearly as many in Williamsburg; of large undivided interests in Milwaukie, Chicago, Rock River, Moonville, and other similar places; besides owning a considerable part of a place called Coney Island. In a word, the landed estate of Henry Halfacre, Esq., '*inventoried*,' as he expressed it, just 2,612,000 dollars; a handsome sum, it must be confessed, for a man who, when he began his beneficent and energetic career in this branch of business, was just 23,417 dollars worse than nothing. It is true, that there was some drawback on all this prosperity, Mr. Halfacre's bonds, notes, mortgages, and other liabilities making a sum total that amounted to the odd 600,000 dollars; this still left him, however, a handsome paper balance of two millions.

Notwithstanding the amount of his 'bills payable,' Mr. Halfacre considered himself a very prudent man: first, because he insisted on having no book debts; second, because he always took another man's paper for a larger amount than he had given of his own, for any specific lot or lots; thirdly, and lastly, because he was careful to 'extend himself,' at the risk of other persons. There is no question, had all his lots been sold as he had inventoried them; had his debts been paid; and had he not spent his money a little faster than it was bona fide made, that Henry Halfacre, Esq. would have been a very rich man. As he managed, however, by means of getting portions of the paper he received discounted, to maintain a fine figure account in the bank, and to pay all current demands, he began to be known as the *rich* Mr. Halfacre. But one of his children, the fair Eudosia, was out;[83] and as she had some distance to make in the better society of the town, ere she could pass for aristocratic, it was wisely determined that a golden bridge should be thrown across the dividing chasm. A hundred-dollar pocket handkerchief, it was hoped, would serve for the keystone, and then all the ends of life would be attained. As to a husband, a pretty girl like Eudosia, and the daughter of a man of 'four figure' lots, might get one any day.

Honor O'Flaherty was both short-legged and short-breathed. She felt the full importance of her mission; and having an extensive acquaintance among the other Milesians of the town, and of her class, she stopped no less than eleven times to communicate the magnitude of Miss Dosie's purchase. To two particular favorites she actually showed me, under solemn promise of secrecy; and to four others she promised a peep some day, after her *bossee* had fairly worn me. In this manner my arrival was circulated prematurely in certain coteries, the pretty mouths and fine voices that spoke of my marvels being quite unconscious that they were circulating news that had reached their ears via Honor O'Flaherty, Biddy Noon, and Kathleen Brady.

Mr. Halfacre occupied a very genteel residence in Broadway, where he and his enjoyed the full benefit of all the dust, noise, and commotion of that great thoroughfare. This house had been purchased and mort-gaged, generally simultaneous operations with this great operator, as soon as he had 'inventoried' half a million. It was a sort of patent of nobility to live in Broadway; and the acquisition of such a residence was like the purchase of a marquiseta in Italy. When Eudosia was fairly in possession of a hundred-dollar pocket handkerchief, the great seal might be said to be attached to the document that was to elevate the Halfacres throughout all future time.

Now the beautiful Eudosia – for beautiful, and even lovely, this glorious-looking creature was, in spite of a very badly modulated voice, certain inroads upon the fitness of things in the way of expression, and a want of a knowledge of the finesse of fine life – now the beautiful Eudosia had an intimate friend named Clara Caverly, who was as unlike her as possible, in character, education, habits, and appearance; and yet who was firmly her friend. The attachment was one of childhood and accident – the two girls having been neighbors and school-fellows until they had got to like each other, after the manner in which young people form such friendships, to wear away under the friction of the world, and the pressure of time. Mr. Caverly was a lawyer of good practice, fair reputation, and respectable family. His wife happened to be a lady from her cradle, and the daughter had experienced the advantage of as great a blessing. Still Mr. Caverly was what the world of New York, in 1832, called poor; that is to say, he had no known bank-stock, did not own a lot on the island, was director of neither bank nor insurance company, and lived in a modest two-story house, in White Street. It is true his practice supported his family, and enabled him to invest in bonds and mortgages two or three thousand a year; and he owned the fee of some fifteen or eighteen farms in Orange County, which were falling in from three-lives leases, and which had been in his family ever since the seventeenth century. But, at a period of prosperity like that which prevailed in 1832, 3, 4, 5, and 6, the hereditary dollar was not worth more than twelve and a half cents, as compared with the 'inventoried' dollar. As there is something, after all, in a historical name, and the Caverlys still had the best of it, in the way of society, Eudosia was permitted to continue the visits in White Street, even after her own family were in full possession in Broadway, and Henry Halfacre, Esq., had got to be enumerated among the Manhattan nabobs. Clara Caverly was in Broadway when Honor O'Flagherty arrived with me, out of breath, in consequence of the shortness of her legs, and the necessity of making up for lost time.

'There, Miss Dosie,' cried the exulting housemaid, for such was Honor's domestic rank, though preferred to so honorable and con-fidential a mission – 'There, Miss Dosie, there it is, and it's a jewel.'

'What has Honor brought you *now*?' asked Clara Caverly in her quiet way, for she saw by the brilliant eyes and flushed cheeks of her friend that it was something the other would have pleasure in convers-ing about. 'You make so many purchases, dear Eudosia, that I should think you would weary of them.'

'What, weary of beautiful dresses? Never, Clara, never! That might do for White Street, but in Broadway one is never tired of such things – see,' laying me out at full length in her lap, 'this is a pocket handkerchief – I wish your opinion of it.'

Clara examined me very closely, and, in spite of something like a frown, and an expression of dissatisfaction that gathered about her pretty face – for Clara was pretty, too – I could detect some of the latent feelings of the sex, as she gazed at my exquisite lace, perfect ornamental work, and unequaled fineness. Still, her education and habits triumphed, and she would not commend what she regarded as ingenuity misspent, and tasteless, because senseless, luxury.

'This handkerchief cost *one hundred dollars*, Clara,' said Eudosia, deliberately and with emphasis, imitating, as near as possible, the tone of Bobbinet & Co.

'Is it possible, Eudosia! What a sum to pay for so useless a thing!'

'Useless! Do you call a pocket handkerchief useless?'

'Quite so, when it is made in a way to render it out of the question to put it to the uses for which it was designed. I should as soon think of trimming gumshoes with satin, as to trim a handkerchief in that style.'

'Style? Yes, I flatter myself it *is* style to have a handkerchief that cost a hundred dollars. Why, Clara Caverly, the highest priced thing of this sort that was ever before sold in New York only came to seventy-nine dollars. Mine is superior to all, by twenty-one dollars!'

Clara Caverly sighed. It was not with regret, or envy, or any unworthy feeling, however; it was a fair, honest, moral sigh, that had its birth in the thought of how much good a hundred dollars might have done, properly applied. It was under the influence of this feeling, too, that she said, somewhat inopportunely it must be confessed, though quite innocently –

'Well, Eudosia, I am glad you can afford such a luxury, at all events. Now is a good time to get your subscription to the Widows' and Orphans' Society. Mrs. Thoughtful has desired me to ask for it half a dozen times; I dare say it has escaped you that you are quite a twelve-month in arrear.'

'*Now* a good time to ask for three dollars! What, just when I've paid a hundred dollars for a pocket handkerchief? That was not said with your usual good sense, my dear. People must be *made* of money to pay out so much at one time.'

'When may I tell Mrs. Thoughtful, then, that you will send it to her?'

'I am sure that is more than I can say. Pa will be in no hurry to give me more money soon, and I want, at this moment, near a hundred dollars' worth of articles of dress to make a decent appearance. The Society can be in no such hurry for its subscriptions; they must amount to a good deal.'

'Not if never paid. Shall I lend you the money – my mother gave me ten dollars this morning, to make a few purchases, which I can very well do without until you can pay me.'

'*Do*, dear girl – you are always one of the best creatures in the world. How much is it? three dollars I believe.'

'Six, if you pay the past and present year. I will pay Mrs. Thoughtful before I go home. But, dear Eudosia, I wish you had not bought that foolish pocket handkerchief.'

'Foolish! Do you call a handkerchief with such lace, and all this magnificent work on it, and which cost a *hundred dollars*, foolish? Is it foolish to have money, or to be thought rich?'

'Certainly not the first, though it may be better not to be thought rich. I wish to see you always dressed with propriety, for you do credit to your dress; but this handkerchief is out of place.'

'Out of place! Now, hear me, Clara, though it is to be a great secret. What do you think Pa is worth?'

'Bless me, these are things I never think of. I do not even know how much my own father is worth. Mother tells me how much I may spend, and I can want to learn no more.'

'Well, Mr. Murray dined with Pa last week, and they sat over their wine until near ten. I overheard them talking, and got into this room to listen, for I thought I should get something new. At first they said nothing but "lots – lots – uptown – downtown – twenty-five feet front – dollar, dollar, dollar." La! child, you never heard such stuff in your life!'

'One gets used to these things, notwithstanding,' observed Clara, drily.

'Yes, one *does* hear a great deal of it. I shall be glad when the gentlemen learn to talk of something else. But the best is to come. At last, Pa asked Mr. Murray if he had inventoried lately.'

'Did he?'

'Yes, he did. Of course you know what that means?'

'It means to *fill*, as they call it, does it not?'

'So I thought at first, but it means no such thing. It means to count up, and set down how much one is worth. Mr. Murray said he did *that* every month, and of course he knew very well what *he* was worth. I forget how much it was, for I didn't care, you know George Murray is not as old as I am, and so I listened to what Pa had inventoried. Now, how much do you guess?'

'Really, my dear, I haven't the least idea,' answered Clara, slightly gaping – 'a thousand dollars, perhaps.'

'A thousand dollars! What, for a gentleman who keeps his coach – lives in Broadway – dresses his daughter as I dress, and gives her hundred-dollar handkerchiefs. Two hundred million, my dear; two hundred million!'

Eudosia had interpolated the word 'hundred' quite innocently, for, as usually happens with those to whom money is new, her imagination ran ahead of her arithmetic. 'Yes,' she added, 'two hundred millions; besides sixty millions of odd money!'

'That sounds like a great deal,' observed Clara quietly; for, besides caring very little for these millions, she had not a profound respect for her friend's accuracy on such subjects.

'It is a great deal. Ma says there are not ten richer men than Pa in the state. Now, does not this alter the matter about the pocket hand-kerchief? It would be mean in me not to have a hundred-dollar handkerchief, when I could get one.'

'It may alter the matter as to the extravagance; but it does not alter it as to the fitness. Of what *use* is a pocket handkerchief like this? A pocket handkerchief is made for *use*, my dear, not for show.'

'You would not have a young lady use her pocket handkerchief like a snuffy old nurse, Clara?'

'I would have her use it like a young lady, and in no other way. But it always strikes me as a proof of ignorance and a want of refinement when the uses of things are confounded. A pocket handkerchief, at the best, is but a menial appliance, and it is bad taste to make it an object of attraction. *Fine*, it may be, for that conveys an idea of delicacy in its owner; but ornamented beyond reason, never. Look what a tawdry and vulgar thing an embroidered slipper is on a woman's foot.'

'Yes, I grant you that, but everybody cannot have hundred-dollar handkerchiefs, though they may have embroidered slippers. I shall wear my purchase at Miss Trotter's ball tonight.'

To this Clara made no objection, though she still looked dis-approbation of her purchase. Now, the lovely Eudosia had not a bad heart; she had only received a bad education. Her parents had given her a smattering of the usual accomplishments, but here her superior instruction ended. Unable to discriminate themselves, for the want of this very education, they had been obliged to trust their daughter to the care of mercenaries, who fancied their duties discharged when they had taught their pupil to repeat like a parrot. All she acquired had been for effect, and not for the purpose of everyday use; in which her instruction and her pocket handkerchief might be said to be of a piece.

11

And here I will digress a moment to make a single remark on a subject of which popular feeling, in America, under the influence of popular habits, is apt to take an ex parte view. Accomplishments are derided as useless, in comparison with what is considered household virtues. The accomplishment of a cook is to make good dishes, of a seamstress to sew well, and of a lady to possess refined tastes, a cultivated mind, and agreeable and intellectual habits. The real *virtues* of all are the same, though subject to laws peculiar to their station; but it is a very different thing when we come to the mere accomplishments. To deride all the refined attainments of human skill denotes ignorance of the means of human happiness, nor is it any evidence of acquaintance with the intricate machinery of social greatness and a lofty civilization. These gradations in attainments are inseparable from civilized society, and if the skill of the ingenious and laborious is indispensable to a solid foundation, without the tastes and habits of the refined and cultivated, it never can be graceful or pleasing.

Eudosia had some indistinct glimmerings of this fact, though it was not often that she came to sound and discriminating decisions even in matters less complicated. In the present instance she saw this truth only by halves, and that, too, in its most commonplace aspect, as will appear by the remark she made on the occasion.

'Then, Clara, as to the *price* I have paid for this handkerchief,' she said, 'you ought to remember what the laws of political economy lay down on such subjects. I suppose your Pa makes you study political economy, my dear?'

'Indeed he does not. I hardly know what it means.'

'Well, that is singular; for Pa says, in this age of the world, it is the only way to be rich. Now, it is by means of a trade in lots, and political economy, generally, that he has succeeded so wonderfully; for, to own the truth to you, Clara, Pa hasn't always been rich.'

'No?' answered Clara, with a half-suppressed smile, she knowing the fact already perfectly well.

'Oh, no – far from it – but we don't speak of this publicly, it being a sort of disgrace in New York, you know, not to be thought worth at least half a million. I dare say your Pa is worth as much as that?'

'I have not the least idea he is worth a fourth of it, though I do not pretend to know. To me half a million of dollars seems a great deal of money, and I know my father considers himself poor – poor, at least, for one of his station. But what were you about to say of political economy? I am curious to hear how *that* can have any thing to do with your handkerchief.'

'Why, my dear, in this manner. You know a distribution of labor is the source of all civilization – that trade is an exchange of equivalents – that custom houses fetter these equivalents – that nothing that is fettered is free – '

'My dear Eudosia, what *is* your tongue running on?'

'You will not deny, Clara, that any thing that is fettered is not free? And that freedom is the greatest blessing of this happy country; and that trade ought to be as free as any thing else?'

All this was gibberish to Clara Caverly, who understood the phrases, notwithstanding, quite as well as the friend who was using them. Political economy is especially a science of terms; and free trade, as a branch of it is called, is just the portion of it which is indebted to them the most. But Clara had not patience to hear any more of the unintelligible jargon which has got possession of the world today, much as Mr. Pitt's celebrated sinking fund scheme for paying off the national debt of Great Britain did,[84] half a century since, and under very much the same influences; and she desired her friend to come at once to the point, as connected with the pocket handkerchief.

'Well, then,' resumed Eudosia, 'it is connected in this way. The luxuries of the rich give employment to the poor, and cause money to circulate. Now this handkerchief of mine, no doubt, has given employment to some poor French girl for four or five months, and, of course, food and raiment. She has earned, no doubt, fifty of the hundred dollars I have paid. Then the custom house – ah, Clara, if it were not for that vile custom house, I might have had the handkerchief for at least five-and-twenty dollars lower – !'

'In which case you would have prized it five-and-twenty times less,' answered Clara, smiling archly.

'*That* is true; yes, free trade, after all, does *not* apply to pocket handkerchiefs.'

'And yet,' interrupted Clara, laughing, 'if one can believe what one reads, it applies to hackney coaches, ferry boats, doctors, lawyers, and even the clergy. My father says it is – '

'What? I am curious to know, Clara, what as plain speaking a man as Mr. Caverly calls it.'

'He is plain speaking enough to call it a – *humbug*,' said the daughter, endeavoring to mouth the word in a theatrical manner. 'But, as Othello says, the handkerchief.'[85]

'Oh! Fifty dollars go to the poor girl who does the work, twenty-five more to the odious custom house, some fifteen to rent, fuel, lights, and ten, perhaps, to Mr. Bobbinet, as profits. Now all this is very good, and very useful to society, as you must own.'

Alas, poor Adrienne! Thou didst not receive for me as many francs as this fair calculation gave thee dollars; and richer wouldst thou have been, and, oh, how much happier, hadst thou kept the money paid for me, sold the lace even at a loss, and spared thyself so many, many hours of painful and anxious toil! But it is thus with human calculations: the propositions seem plausible, and the reasoning fair, while stern truth lies behind all to level the pride of understanding, and prove the fallacy of the wisdom of men. The reader may wish to see how closely Eudosia's account of profit and loss came to the fact, and I shall, consequently, make up the statement from the private books of the firm that had the honor of once owning me, viz.:

Super-extraordinary Pocket handkerchief, &c., in account with Bobbinet & Co.

DR.

To money paid, first cost, francs 100, at 5.25 – $19.04
To interest on same for ninety days, at 7 percent – 00.33
To portion of passage money – 00.04
To porterage – 00.00 1/4
To washing and making up – 00.25

– – – – – –

$19.66 1/4

CR.

By cash paid by Miss Thimble – $1.00
By cash paid for article – 100.00
By washerwoman's deduction – 00.05

– – – – – –

101.05

– – – – – –

By profit – $81.39 ?

As Clara Caverly had yet to see Mrs. Thoughtful, and pay Eudosia's subscription, the former now took her leave. I was thus left alone with my new employer, for the first time, and had an opportunity of learning something of her true character, without the interposition of third persons; for, let a friend have what hold he or she may on your heart, it has a few secrets that are strictly its own. If admiration of myself could win my favor, I had every reason to be satisfied with the hands into which fortune had now thrown me. There were many things to admire in Eudosia – a defective education being the great evil with which she had to contend. Owing to this education, if it really deserved such a name, she had superficial accomplishments, superficially acquired – principles that scarce extended beyond the *retenue* [86] and morals of her sex – tastes that had been imbibed from questionable models – and hopes that proceeded from a false estimate of the very false position into which she had been accidentally and suddenly thrown. Still Eudosia had a heart. She could scarcely be a woman, and escape the influence of this portion of the female frame. By means of the mesmeritic power of a pocket handkerchief, I soon discovered that there was a certain Morgan Morely in New York, to whom she longed to exhibit my perfection, as second to the wish to exhibit her own.

I scarcely know whether to felicitate myself or not, on the circumstance that I was brought out the very first evening I passed in the possession of Eudosia Halfacre. The beautiful girl was dressed and ready for Mrs. Trotter's ball by eight; and her admiring mother thought it impossible for the heart of Morgan Morely, a reputed six-figure fortune, to hold out any longer. By some accident or other, Mr. Halfacre did not appear – he had not dined at home; and the two females had all the joys of anticipation to themselves.

'I wonder what has become of your father,' said Mrs. Halfacre, after inquiring for her husband for the tenth time. 'It is so like him to forget an engagement to a ball. I believe he thinks of nothing but his lots. It is really a great trial, Dosie, to be so rich. I sometimes wish we weren't worth more than a million, for, after all, I suspect true happiness is to be found in these little fortunes. Heigho! It's ten o'clock, and we must go, if we mean to be there at all; for Mrs. Caverly once said, in my presence, that she thought it as vulgar to be too late, as too early.'

The carriage was ordered, and we all three got in, leaving a message for Mr. Halfacre to follow us. As the rumor that a 'three-figure' pocket handkerchief was to be at the ball had preceded my appearance, a general buzz announced my arrival in the *salle à manger-salons*[87]. I have no intention of describing fashionable society in the GREAT EMPORIUM of the *western world*. Everybody understands that it is on the best possible footing – grace, ease, high breeding and common sense being so blended together, that it is exceedingly difficult to analyze them, or, indeed, to tell which is which. It is this moral fusion that renders the whole perfect, as the harmony of fine coloring throws a glow of glory on the pictures of Claude, or, for that matter, on those of Cole, too.[88] Still, as envious and evil-disposed persons have dared to call in question the elegance, and more especially the *retenue* of a Manhattanese rout, I feel myself impelled, if not by that high sentiment, patriotism, at least by a feeling of gratitude for the great consideration that is attached to pocket handkerchiefs, just to declare that it is all scandal. If I have any fault to find with New York society, it is on account of its formal and almost priggish quiet – the female voice being usually quite lost in it – thus leaving a void in the ear, not to say the heart, that is painful to endure. Could a few young ladies, too, be persuaded to become a little more prominent, and quit their mother's apron strings, it would add vastly to the grouping, and relieve the stiffness of the 'shin-pieces' of formal rows of dark-looking men, and of the flounces of pretty women. These two slight faults repaired, New York society might rival that of Paris; especially in the Chausse d'Autin. More than this I do not wish to say, and less than this I cannot in honor write, for I have made some of the warmest and truest-hearted friends in New York that it ever fell to the lot of a pocket handkerchief to enjoy.

It has been said that my arrival produced a general buzz. In less than a minute Eudosia had made her curtsy, and was surrounded, in a corner, by a bevy of young friends, all silent together, and all dying to see me. To deny the deep gratification I felt at the encomiums I received, would be hypocrisy. They went from my borders to my center – from the lace to the hem – and from the hem to the minutest fiber of my exquisite texture. In a word, I was the first hundred-dollar pocket handkerchief that had then appeared in their circles; and had I been a Polish count, with two sets of moustaches, I could not have been more flattered and 'entertained.' My fame soon spread through the rooms, as two little apartments, with a door between them that made each an alcove of the other, were called; and even the men, the young ones in particular, began to take an interest in me. This latter interest, it is true, did not descend to the minutiae of trimmings and work, or even of fineness, but the 'three figure' had a surprising effect. An elderly lady sent to borrow me for a moment. It was a queer thing to borrow a pocket handkerchief, some will think; but I was lent to twenty people that night; and while in her hands, I overheard the following little aside, between two young fashionables, who were quite unconscious of the acuteness of the senses of our family.

'This must be a rich old chap, this Halfacre, to be able to give his daughter a hundred-dollar pocket handkerchief, Tom; one might do well to get introduced.'

'If you'll take my advice, Ned, you'll keep where you are,' was the answer. 'You've been to the surrogate's office, and have seen the will of old Simonds, and *know* that he has left his daughter 78,000 dollars; and, after all, this pocket handkerchief may be only a sign. I always distrust people who throw out such lures.'

'Oh, rely on it, there is no sham here; Charley Pray told me of this girl last week, when no one had ever heard of her pocket handkerchief.'

'Why don't Charley, then, take her himself? I'm sure, if I had *his* imperial, I could pick and choose among all the second-class heiresses in town.'

'Ay, there's the rub, Tom; one is obliged in our business to put up with the *second* class. Why can't we aim higher at once, and get such girls as the Burtons, for instance?'

'The Burtons have, or have had, a mother.'

'And haven't all girls mothers? Who ever heard of a man or a woman without a mother!'

'True, physically; but I mean morally. Now this very Eudosia Halfacre has no more mother, in the last sense, than you have a wet nurse. She has an old woman to help her make a fool of herself; but, in the way of a mother, she would be better off with a pair of good gumshoes. A creature that is just to tell a girl not to wet her feet, and when to cloak and uncloak, and to help tear the checkbook out of money, is no more of a mother than old Simonds was of a Solomon, when he made that will that every one of us knows by heart quite as well as he knows the constitution.'

Here a buzz in the room drew the two young men a little aside, and for a minute I heard nothing but indistinct phrases, in which 'removal of deposits,' 'panic,' 'General Jackson,' and 'revolution,' were the only words I could fairly understand.[89] Presently, however, the young men dropped back into their former position, and the dialogue proceeded.

'There!' exclaimed Ned, in a voice louder than was prudent, '*that* is what I call an escape! That cursed handkerchief was very near taking me in. I call it swindling to make such false pretensions.'

'It might be very awkward with one who was not properly on his guard; but with the right sort there is very little danger.'

Here the two *élégants*[90] led out a couple of heiresses to dance; and I heard no more of them or of their escapes. Lest the reader, however, should be misled, I wish to add, that these two worthies are not to be taken as specimens of New York morality at all – no place on earth being more free from fortune-hunters, or of a higher tone of social morals in this delicate particular. As I am writing for American readers, I wish to say, that all they are told of the vices of *old* countries, on the other side of the Atlantic, is strictly true; while all that is said, directly, or by implication, of the vices and faults of this happy young country, is just so much calumny. The many excellent friends I have made, since my arrival in this hemisphere, have bound my heart to them to all eternity; and I will now proceed with my philosophical and profound disquisitions on what I have seen, with a perfect confidence that I shall receive credit, and an independence of opinion that is much too dear to me to consent to place it in question. But to return to facts.

I was restored to Eudosia, with a cold, reserved look, by a lady into whose hands I had passed, which struck me as singular, as shown to the owner of such an article. It was not long, however, before I discovered, to use a homely phrase, that something had happened; and I was not altogether without curiosity to know what that something was. It was apparent enough that Eudosia was the subject of general observation, and of general conversation, though, so long as she held me in her hand, it exceeded all my acuteness of hearing to learn what was said. The poor girl fancied her pocket handkerchief was the common theme; and in this she was not far from right, though it was in a way she little suspected. At length Clara Caverly drew near, and borrowed me of her friend, under a pretext of showing me to her mother, who was in the room, though, in fact, it was merely to get me out of sight; for Clara was much too well bred to render any part of another's dress the subject of her discussions in general society. As if impatient to get me out of sight, I was thrown on a sofa, among a little pile of *consoeurs*[91] (if there is such a word), for a gathering had been made, while our pretty hostesses were dancing, in order to compare our beauty. There we lay quite an hour, a congress of pocket handkerchiefs, making our comments on the company, and gossiping in our own fashion. It was only the next day that I discovered the reason we were thus neglected; for, to own the truth, something had occurred that suddenly brought 'three-figure,' and even 'two-figure' people of our class into temporary disrepute. I shall explain that reason at the proper moment.

The conversation among the handkerchiefs on the sofa ran principally on the subject of our comparative market value. I soon discovered that there was a good deal of envy against me, on account of my 'three figures,' although, I confess, I thought I cut a 'poor figure,' lying as I did, neglected in a corner, on the very first evening of my appearance in the fashionable world. But some of the opinions uttered on this occasion – always in the mesmeritic manner, be it remembered – will be seen in the following dialogue.

'Well!' exclaimed $25, 'this is the first ball I have been at that I was not thought good enough to have a place in the quadrille. You see all the canaille are in the hands of their owners, while we, the elite of pocket handkerchiefs, are left here in a corner, like so many cloaks.'

'There must be a reason for this, certainly,' answered $45, 'though *you* have been flourished about these two winters, in a way that ought to satisfy one of YOUR pretensions.'

An animated reply was about to set us all in commotion, when $80, who, next to myself, had the highest claims of any in the party, changed the current of feeling, by remarking –

'It is no secret that we are out of favor for a night or two, in consequence of three figures having been paid for one of us, this very day, by a bossess, whose father stopped payment within three hours after he signed the check that was to pay the importer. I overheard the whole story, half an hour since, and thus, you see, everyone is afraid to be seen with an aristocratic handkerchief, just at this moment. But – bless you! in a day or two all will be forgotten, and we shall come more into favor than ever. All is always forgotten in New York in a week.'

Such was, indeed, the truth. One General Jackson had 'removed the deposits,' as I afterwards learned, though I never could understand exactly what that meant; but, it suddenly made money scarce, more especially with those who had none; and every body that was 'extended' began to quake in their shoes.[92] Mr. Halfacre happened to be in this awkward predicament, and he broke down in the effort to sustain himself. His energy had overreached itself, like the tumbler who breaks his neck in throwing seventeen hundred somersaults backwards.

12

Every one is more apt to hear an unpleasant rumor than those whom it immediately affects. Thus Eudosia and her mother were the only persons at Mrs. Trotter's ball who were ignorant of what had happened; one whispering the news to another, though no one could presume to communicate the fact to the parties most interested. In a commercial town, like New York, the failure of a reputed millionaire could not long remain a secret, and everybody stared at the wife and daughter, and me; first, as if they had never seen the wives and daughters of bankrupts before; and second, as if they had never seen them surrounded by the evidences of their extravagance.

But the crisis was at hand, and the truth could not long be concealed. Eudosia was permitted to cloak and get into the carriage unaided by any beau, a thing that had not happened to her since speculation had brought her father into notice. The circumstance, more than any other, attracted her attention; and the carriage no sooner started than the poor girl gave vent to her feelings.

'What *can* be the matter, Ma?' Eudosia said, 'that every person in Mrs. Trotter's rooms should stare so at me, this evening? I am sure my dress is as well made and proper as that of any other young lady in the rooms, and as for the handkerchief, I could see envy in fifty eyes, when their owners heard the price.'

'That is all, dear – they *did* envy you, and no wonder they stared – nothing makes people stare like envy. I thought this handkerchief would make a commotion. Oh! I used to stare myself when envious.'

'Still it was odd that Morgan Morely did not ask me to dance – he knows how fond I am of dancing, and for the credit of so beautiful a handkerchief, he ought to have been more than usually attentive tonight.'

Mrs. Halfacre gaped, and declared that she was both tired and sleepy, which put an end to conversation until the carriage reached her own door.

Both Mrs. Halfacre and Eudosia were surprised to find the husband and father still up. He was pacing the drawing room, by the light of a single tallow candle, obviously in great mental distress.

'Bless me!' exclaimed the wife – '*you* up at this hour? – what *can* have happened? what *has* come to our door?'

'Nothing but beggary,' answered the man, smiling with a bitterness that showed he felt an inhuman joy, at that fierce moment, in making others as miserable as himself. 'Yes, Mrs. Henry Halfacre – yes, Miss Eudosia Halfacre, you are both beggars – I hope that, at least, will satisfy you.'

'You mean, Henry, that you have failed?' For that was a word too familiar in New York not to be understood even by the ladies. 'Tell me the worst at once – is it true, *have* you failed?'

'It *is* true – I *have* failed. My notes have been this day protested for 95,000 dollars, and I have not ninety-five dollars in bank. Tomorrow, 23,000 more will fall due, and this month will bring round quite 130,000 more. That accursed removal of the deposits, and that tiger, Jackson, have done it all.'

To own the truth, both the ladies were a little confounded. They wept, and for some few minutes there was a dead silence, but curiosity soon caused them both to ask questions.

'This is very dreadful, and with our large family!' commenced the mother – 'and so the general has it all to answer for – why did you let him give so many notes for you?'

'No – no – it is not that – I gave the notes myself; but he removed the deposits, I tell you.'

'It's just like him, the old wretch! To think of his removing your deposits, just as you wanted them so much yourself! But why did the clerks at the bank let him have them – they ought to have known that you had all this money to pay, and people cannot well pay debts without money.'

'You are telling that, my dear, to one who knows it by experience. That is the very reason why I have failed. I have a great many debts, and I have no money.'

'But you have hundreds of lots – give them lots, Henry, and that will settle all your difficulties. You must remember how all our friends have envied us our lots.'

'Aye, no fear, but they'll get the lots, my dear – unless, indeed,' added the speculator, 'I take good care to prevent it. Thank God! I'm not a *declared* bankrupt. I can yet make my own assignee.'

'Well, then, I wouldn't say a word about it – declare nothing, and let 'em find out that you have failed, in the best manner they can. Why tell people your distresses, so that they may pity you. I hate pity, above all things – and especially the pity of my own friends.'

'Oh, that will be dreadful!' put in Eudosia. 'For Heaven's sake, Pa, don't let anybody pity us.'

'Very little fear of that, I fancy,' muttered the father; 'people who shoot up like rockets, in two or three years, seldom lay the foundations of much pity in readiness for their fall.'

'Well, I declare, Dosie, this is *too* bad in the old general, after all. I'm sure it *must* be unconstitutional for a president to remove your father's deposits. If I were in your place, Mr. Halfacre, I wouldn't fail just to spite them. You know you always said that a man of energy can do any thing in this country; and I have heard Mr. Munny say that he didn't know a man of greater energy than yourself.'

The grin with which the ruined speculator turned on his wife was nearly sardonic.

'Your men of energy are the very fellows *to* fail,' he said; 'however, they shall find if I have had extraordinary energy in running into debt, that I have extraordinary energy, too, in getting out of it. Mrs. Halfacre, we must quit this house this very week, and all this fine furniture must be brought to the hammer. I mean to preserve my character, at least.'

This was said loftily, and with the most approved accents.

'Surely it isn't necessary to move to do that, my dear! Other people fail, and keep their houses, and furniture, and carriages, and such other things. Let us not make ourselves the subjects of unpleasant remarks.'

'I intend that as little as you do yourself. We must quit this house and bring the furniture under the hammer, or part with all those lots you so much esteem and prize.'

'Oh! If the house and furniture will pay the notes I'm content, especially if you can contrive to keep the lots. Dosie will part with her handkerchief, too, I dare say, if that will do any good.'

'By George! that will be a capital idea – yes, the handkerchief must be sent back tomorrow morning; *that* will make a famous talk. I only bought it because Munny was present, and I wanted to get 50,000 dollars out of him, to meet this crisis. The thing didn't succeed; but, no matter, the handkerchief will tell in settling up. That handkerchief, Dosie, may be made to cover a hundred lots.'

In what manner I was to open so much, like the tent of the Arabian Nights, was a profound mystery to me then, as well as it was to the ladies; but the handsome Eudosia placed me in her father's hand with a frank liberality that proved she was not altogether without good qualities. As I afterwards discovered, indeed, these two females had most of the excellences of a devoted wife and daughter, their frivolities being the result of vicious educations or of no educations at all, rather than of depraved hearts. When Mr. Halfacre went into liquidation, as it is called, and compromised with his creditors, reserving to himself a pretty little capital of some eighty or a hundred thousand dollars, by means of judicious payments to confidential creditors, his wife and daughter saw all *they* most prized taken away, and the town was filled with the magnitude of their sacrifices, and with the handsome manner in which both submitted to make them. By this ingenious device, the insolvent not only preserved his character, by no means an unusual circumstance in New York, however, but he preserved about half of his bona fide estate also, his creditors, as was customary, doing the *paying*.

It is unnecessary to dwell on the remainder of this dialogue, my own adventures so soon carrying me into an entirely different sphere. The following morning, however, as soon as he had breakfasted, Mr. Halfacre put me in his pocket, and walked down the street, with the port of an afflicted and stricken, but thoroughly honest man. When he reached the shop door of Bobbinet & Co., he walked boldly in, and laid me on the counter with a flourish so meek, that even the clerks, a very matter-of-fact caste in general, afterwards commented on it.

'Circumstances of an unpleasant nature, on which I presume it is unnecessary to dwell, compel me to offer you this handkerchief back again, gentlemen,' he said, raising his hand to his eyes in a very affecting manner. 'As a bargain is a bargain, I feel great reluctance to disturb its sacred obligations, but I *cannot* suffer a child of mine to retain such a luxury, while a single individual can justly say that I owe him a dollar.'

'What fine sentiments!' said Silky, who was lounging in a corner of the shop – 'wonderful sentiments, and such as become a man of honesty.'

Those around the colonel approved of his opinion, and Mr. Halfacre raised his head like one who was not afraid to look his creditors in the face.

'I approve of your motives, Mr. Halfacre,' returned Bobbinet, 'but you know the character of the times, and the dearness of rents. That article has been seen in private hands, doubtless, and can no longer be considered fresh – we shall be forced to make a considerable abatement, if we consent to comply.'

'Name your own terms, sir; so they leave me a single dollar for my creditors, I shall be happy.'

'Wonderful sentiments!' repeated the colonel – 'we must send that man to the national councils!'

After a short negotiation, it was settled that Mr. Halfacre was to receive $50, and Bobbinet & Co. were to replace me in their drawer. The next morning an article appeared in a daily paper of pre-eminent honesty and truth, and talents, in the following words: –

Worthy of Imitation. – A distinguished gentleman of this city, H — H — , Esquire, having been compelled to *suspend*, in consequence of the late robbery of the Bank of the United States by the cold-blooded miscreant whose hoary head disgraces the White House, felt himself bound to return an article of dress, purchased as recently as yesterday by his lovely daughter, and who, in every respect, was entitled to wear it, as she would have adorned it, receiving back the price, with a view to put it in the fund he is already collecting to meet the demands of his creditors. It is due to the very respectable firm of Bobbinet & Co. to add, that it refunded the money with the greatest liberality, at the first demand. We can recommend this house to our readers as one of the most liberal in OUR city (by the way the editor who wrote this article didn't own a foot of the town, or of anything else) and as possessing a very large and well-selected assortment of the choicest goods.

The following words – 'we take this occasion to thank Messrs. Bobbinet & Co. for a specimen of most beautiful gloves sent us,' had a line run through in the manuscript, a little reflection telling the learned editor that it might be indiscreet to publish the fact at that precise moment. The American will know how to appreciate the importance of this opinion, in relation to the house in question, when he is told that it was written by one of those inspired moralists, and profound constitutional lawyers, and ingenious political economists, who daily teach their fellow creatures how to give practical illustrations of the mandates of the Bible, how to discriminate in vexed questions arising from the national compact, and how to manage their private affairs in such a way as to escape the quicksands that have wrecked their own.

As some of my readers may feel an interest in the fate of poor Eudosia, I will take occasion to say, before I proceed with the account of my own fortunes, that it was not half as bad as might have been supposed. Mr. Halfacre commenced his compromises under favorable auspices. The reputation of the affair of the pocket handkerchief was of great service, and creditors relented as they thought of the hardship of depriving a pretty girl of so valuable an appliance. Long before the public had ceased to talk about the removal of the deposits, Mr. Halfacre had arranged every thing to his own satisfaction. The lots were particularly useful, one of them paying off a debt that had been contracted for half a dozen. Now and then he met an obstinate fellow who insisted on his money, and who talked of suits in chancery. Such men were paid off in full, litigation being the speculator's aversion. As for the fifty dollars received for me, it answered to go to market with until other funds were found. This diversion of the sum from its destined object, however, was apparent rather than real, since food was indispensable to enable the excellent but unfortunate man to work for the benefit of his creditors. In short, every thing was settled in the most satisfactory manner, Mr. Halfacre paying a hundred cents in the dollar, in lots, however, but in such a manner as balanced his books beautifully.

'Now, thank God! I owe no man a sixpence,' said Mr. to Mrs. Halfacre, the day all was concluded, 'and only one small mistake has been made by me, in going through so many complicated accounts, and for such large sums.'

'I had hoped *all* was settled,' answered the good woman in alarm. 'It is that unreasonable man, John Downright, who gives you the trouble, I dare say.'

'He – oh! he is paid in full. I offered him, at first, twenty-five cents in the dollar, but *that* he wouldn't hear to. Then I found a small error, and offered forty. It wouldn't do, and I had to pay the scamp a hundred. I can look that fellow in the face with a perfectly clear conscience.'

'Who else can it be, then?'

'Only your brother, Myers, my dear; somehow or other, we made a mistake in our figures, which made out a demand in his favor of $100,000. I paid it in property, but when we came to look over the figures it was discovered that a cipher too much had been thrown in, and Myers paid back the difference like a man, as he is.'

'And to whom will that difference belong?'

'To whom – oh! – why, of course, to the right owner.'

13

When I found myself once more in the possession of Bobbinet & Co., I fancied that I might anticipate a long residence in their drawers, my freshness, as an article, having been somewhat tarnished by the appearance at Mrs. Trotter's ball. In this I was mistaken, the next day bringing about a release, and a restoration to my proper place in society.

The very morning after I was again in the drawer, a female voice was heard asking for 'worked French pocket handkerchiefs.' As I clearly came within this category – alas, poor Adrienne! – in half a minute I found myself, along with fifty fellows or fellowesses, lying on the counter. The instant I heard the voice, I knew that the speaker was not 'mamma,' but 'my child,' and I now saw that she was fair. Julia Monson was not as brilliantly handsome as my late owner, but she had more feeling and refinement in the expression of her countenance. Still there was an uneasy worldly glancing of the eye, which denoted how much she lived out of herself, in the less favorable understanding of the term; an expression of countenance that I have had occasion to remark in most of those who think a very expensive handkerchief necessary to their happiness. It is, in fact, the natural indication that the mind dwells more on show than on substantial things, and a proof that the possessor of this quality is not content to rely altogether on the higher moral feelings and attainments for her claims to deference. In a word, it is some such trait as that which distinguishes the beautiful plumage of the peacock from the motive that incites the bird to display his feathers.

In company with Miss Monson was another young lady of about her own age, and of a very similar appearance as to dress and station. Still, a first glance discovered an essential difference in character. This companion, who was addressed as Mary, and whose family name was Warren, had none of the uneasiness of demeanor that belonged to her friend, and obviously cared less what others thought of every thing she said or did. When the handkerchiefs were laid on the counter, Julia Monson seized on one with avidity, while Mary Warren regarded us all with a look of cold indifference, if not one of downright displeasure.

'What beauties!' exclaimed the first, the clerk at that moment quitting them to hand some gloves to another customer – 'What delightful needlework! Mary, do *you* purchase one to keep me in countenance, and I will purchase another. I know your mother gave you the money this very morning.'

'Not for that object, Julia. My dear mother little thinks I shall do any such thing.'

'And why not? A rich pocket handkerchief is a stylish thing!'

'I question if style, as you call it, is just the thing for a young woman, under any circumstances; but, to confess the truth, I think a pocket handkerchief that is to be *looked* at and which is not to be *used*, vulgar.'

'Not in Sir Walter Scott's[93] signification, my dear,' answered Julia laughing, 'for it is not so very *common*. Everybody cannot have a worked French pocket handkerchief.'

'Sir Walter Scott's definition of what is vulgar is open to criticism, I fancy. The word comes from the common mind, or common practices, beyond a question, but it now means what is common as opposed to what is cultivated and refined. It is an absurdity, too, to make a thing respectable because it is common. A fib is one of the commonest things in the world, and yet it is scarcely respectable.'

'Oh! Every one says you are a philosoph*eress*, Mary, and I ought to have expected some such answer. But a handkerchief I am determined to have, and it shall be the very handsomest I can find.'

'And the *dearest*? Well, you will have a very ladylike wardrobe with one pocket handkerchief in it! I wonder you do not purchase a single shoe.'

'Because I have *two* feet,' replied Julia with spirit, though she laughed good-naturedly – 'but here is the clerk, and he must not hear our quarrels. Have the goodness, sir, to show me the handsomest pocket handkerchief in your shop.'

I was drawn from beneath the pile and laid before the bright black eyes of Julia, with an air of solemn dignity, by the young dealer in finery.

'That, ma'am,' he said, 'is the very finest and most elegant article not only that *we* have, but which is to be found in America. It was brought out by "our Mr. Silky," the last voyage; *he* said *Paris* cannot produce its equal.'

'This is beautiful, sir, one must admit! What is the price?'

'Why, ma'am, we *ought* in justice to ourselves to have $120 for that article; but, to our regular customers I believe Mr. Bobbinet has determined to ask *only* $100.'

This sounded exceedingly liberal – to ask *only* $100 for that for which there was a sort of moral obligation to ask $120! – and Julia having come out with the intent to throw away a hundred-dollar note that her mother had given her that morning, the bargain was concluded. I was wrapped up carefully in paper, put into Miss Monson's muff, and once more took my departure from the empire of Col. Silky. I no longer occupied a false position.

'Now, I hope you are happy, Julia,' quietly observed Mary Warren, as the two girls took their seats side by side in Mrs. Monson's chariot. 'The surprise to me is, that you forgot to purchase this *ne plus ultra* of elegance while in Paris last summer.'

'My father said he could not afford it; we spent a great deal of money, as you may suppose, in running about, seeing sights, and laying in curiosities, and when I hinted the matter to my mother, she said we must wait until another half year's rents had come round. After all, Mary, there is *one* person at home to whom I shall be ashamed to show this purchase.'

'At home! – is there, indeed? Had you merely said "in town" I could have understood you. Your father and mother approving of what you have done, I do not see who there is *at home* to alarm you.'

Julia blushed when her friend said 'in town,' and her conscious feelings immediately conjured up the image of a certain Betts Shoreham, as the person in her companion's mind's eye. I detected it all easily enough, being actually within six inches of her throbbing heart at that very moment, though concealed in the muff.

'It is not what you suppose, Mary, nor *whom* you suppose,' answered my mistress; 'I mean Mademoiselle Hennequin – I confess I *do* dread the glance of her reproving eye.'

'It is odd enough that you should dread reproval from the governess of your sisters when you do not dread it from your own mother! But Mademoiselle Hennequin has nothing to do with you. You were educated and out before she entered your family, and it is singular that a person not older than yourself, who was engaged in Paris so recently, should have obtained so much influence over the mind of one who never was her pupil.'

'I am not afraid of her in most things,' rejoined Julia, 'but I confess I am in all that relates to taste; particularly in what relates to extravagance.'

'I have greatly misunderstood the character of Mademoiselle Hennequin if she ventured to interfere with you in either! A governess ought not to push her control beyond her proper duties.'

'Nor has Mademoiselle Hennequin,' answered Julia honestly. 'Still I cannot but hear the lessons she gives my sisters, and – yes – to own the truth, I dread the glance she cannot avoid throwing on my purchase. It will say, "of what use are all my excellent lessons in taste and prudence, if an elder sister's example is to counteract them?" It is *that* I dread.'

Mary was silent for fully a minute; then she smiled archly, as girls will smile when certain thoughts cross their playful imaginations, and continued the discourse.

'And Betts Shoreham has nothing to do with all this dread?'

'What is Betts Shoreham to me, or what am I to Betts Shoreham? I am sure the circumstances that we happened to come from Europe in the same packet, and that he continues to visit us now we are at home, do not entitle him to have a veto, as they call it, on my wardrobe.'

'Not *yet*, certainly, my dear. Still they may entitle him to have this veto, *in petto*.'[94]

84

I thought a shade passed over the features of the pretty Julia Monson as she answered her friend, with a seriousness to show that she was now in earnest, and with a propriety that proved she had great good sense at bottom, as well as strong womanly feeling.

'If I have learned nothing else by visiting Europe,' she said, 'I have learned to see how inconsiderate we girls are in America, in talking so much, openly, of this sort of thing. A woman's delicacy is like that of a tender flower, and it must suffer by having her name coupled with that of any man, except him that she is to marry.'

'Julia, dear, I will never speak of Mr. Shoreham again. I should not have done it now had I not thought his attentions were acceptable to you, as I am sure they are to your parents. Certainly, they are *very* marked – at least, so others think as well as myself.'

'I know it *seems* so to the *world*,' answered Julia in a subdued, thoughtful tone, 'but it scarcely seems so to *me*. Betts Shoreham is very agreeable, every way a suitable connection for any of us, and that is the reason people are so ready to fancy him in earnest.'

'In earnest! If Mr. Shoreham pays attentions that are pointed, and is not in earnest, he is a very different person from what I took him to be.'

Julia's voice grew still more gentle, and it was easy enough to see that her feelings were enlisted in the subject.

'It is no more than justice to Betts Shoreham,' she continued, 'to say that he has *not* been pointed in his attentions to *me*. We females are said to be quick in discovering such matters, and I am not more blind than the rest of our sex. He is a young man of good family, and has some fortune, and that makes him welcome in most houses in town, while he is agreeable, well-looking, and thoroughly amiable. He met us abroad, and it is natural for him to keep up an intimacy that recalls pleasant recollections. You will remember, Mary, that before he can be accused of trifling, he must trifle. I think him far more attentive to my mother, my father – nay, to my two little sisters – than he is to *me*. Even Mademoiselle Hennequin is quite as much if not more of a favorite than I am!'

As Mary Warren saw that her friend was serious she changed the subject; soon after, we were set down at Mr. Monson's door. Here the friends parted, Mary Warren preferring to walk home, while Julia and I entered the house together.

'Well, mother,' cried Julia, as she entered Mrs. Monson's room, 'I have found the most beautiful thing you ever beheld, and have bought it. Here it is; what do you think of my choice?'

Mrs. Monson was a kind-hearted, easy, indulgent parent, who had brought her husband a good fortune, and who had married rich in the bargain. Accustomed all her life to a free use of money, and of her own money, too (for this is a country in which very many persons cast the substance of *others* right and left), and when her eldest daughter expressed a wish to possess an elaborate specimen of our race, she had consented from a pure disinclination to deny her child any gratification that might be deemed innocent. Still, she knew that prudence was a virtue, and that Julia had thrown away money that might have been much better employed.

'This is certainly a very beautiful handkerchief,' observed the mother, after examining me carefully, and with somewhat of the manner of a connoisseur, 'surprisingly beautiful; and yet I almost wish, my child, you had not purchased it. A hundred dollars sounds frightfully *en prince*[95] for us poor simple people, who live in nutshells of houses, five and twenty feet front, and fifty-six deep, to pay for a pocket handkerchief. The jewel-box of a young lady who has such handkerchiefs ought to cost thousands, to be in keeping.'

'But, mother, I have only *one*, you will remember, and so my jewels may be limited to hundreds.'

'*One* pocket handkerchief has a mean sound, too. Even one hat is not very superfluous.'

'That is *so* like Mary Warren, mother. If you did not wish me to make the purchase, you had only to say it; I am sure your wish would have been my law.'

'I know it, love; and I am afraid it is your dutiful behavior that has made me careless, in this instance. Your happiness and interests are ever uppermost in my mind, and sometimes they seem to conflict. What young man will dare to choose a wife from among young ladies who expend so much money on their pocket handkerchiefs?'

This was said smilingly, but there was a touch of tenderness and natural concern in the voice and manner of the speaker that made an impression on the daughter.

'I am afraid now, mother, you are thinking of Betts Shoreham,' said Julia, blushing, though she struggled powerfully to appear unconcerned. 'I do not know *why* it is, but both you and Mary Warren appear to be always thinking of Mr. Shoreham.'

The mother smiled; and she was not quite ingenuous when she said in answer to the remark, 'Shoreham was not in my mouth; and you ought not to suppose he was in my mind. Nevertheless, I do not believe he would admire you, or anyone else, the more for being the owner of so expensive an article of dress. He is wealthy, but very prudent in his opinions and habits.'

'Betts Shoreham was born to an estate, and his father before him,' said Julia firmly; 'and such men know how to distinguish between the cant of economy, and those elegancies of life that become people of refinement.'

'No one can better understand the difference between cant in economy as well as cant in some other things, and true taste as well as true morals, than young Shoreham; but there are indulgences that become persons in no class.'

'After all, mother, we are making a trifle a very serious matter. It is but a pocket handkerchief.'

'Very true, my love; and it cost *only* one hundred dollars, and so we'll say no more about it, *bien entendu*[96] that you are not to purchase six dozen at the same price.'

This terminated the dialogue, Julia retiring to her own room, carrying me with her. I was thrown upon the bed, and soon after my mistress opened a door, and summoned her two younger sisters, who were studying on the same floor, to join her. I shall not repeat all the delightful exclamations, and other signs of approbation, that so naturally escaped the two pretty little creatures, to whom I may be said to have now been introduced, when my beauty came under examination. I do not thus speak of myself out of any weakness, for pocket handkerchiefs are wholly without vanity, but simply because I am impelled to utter nothing but truth. Julia had too much consideration to let her young sisters into the secret of my price – for this would have been teaching a premature lesson in extravagance; but, having permitted them to gratify their curiosity, she exacted of them both promises not to speak of me to their governess.

'But why not, Julia?' asked the inquisitive little Jane, 'Mademoiselle Hennequin is so good and so kind, that she would be glad to hear of your good fortune.'

Julia had an indistinct view of her own motive, but she could not avow it to anyone, not even to herself. Jealousy would be too strong, perhaps too indelicate a word, but she alone had detected Betts Shoreham's admiration of the governess; and it was painful to her to permit one who stood in this relation to her own weakness in favor of the young man to be a witness of an act of extravagance to which she had only half consented in committing it, and of which she already more than half repented. From the first, therefore, she determined that Mlle Hennequin should never see me.

14

And now comes an exhibition of my mesmeritic powers, always 'handkerchiefly speaking,' that may surprise those who have not attended to the modern science of invisible fluids. It is by this means, however, that I am enabled to perceive a great deal of that which passes under the roof where I may happen to be, without absolutely seeing it. Much escapes me, of course – for even a pocket handkerchief cannot hear or see every thing; but enough is learned to enable me to furnish a very clear outline of that which occurs near me, more especially if it happens to be within walls of brick. In wooden edifices I find my powers much diminished – the fluids, doubtless, escaping through the pores of the material.

That evening, then, at the usual hour, and while I lay snugly ensconced in a most fragrant and convenient drawer, among various other beings of my species, though not of my family, alas! the inmates of the house assembled in the front drawing room to take a few cups of tea. Mr. and Mrs. Monson, with their only son, John Monson, their three daughters, the governess, and Betts Shoreham, were all present, the latter having dropped in with a new novel for the ladies.

'I do really wish one could see a little advance in the way of real refinement and true elegance among all the vast improvements we are making in frippery and follies,' cried Mr. Monson, throwing down an evening paper in a pettish manner, which sufficiently denoted discontent. 'We are always puffing our own progress in America, without exactly knowing whether a good deal of the road is not to be traveled over again, by way of undoing much that we have done. Here, now, is a specimen of our march in folly, in an advertisement of Bobbinet's, who has pocket handkerchiefs at $75.'

'By the dozen, or by the gross, sir?' demanded Betts Shoreham, quickly.

'Oh, singly – seventy-five dollars each.'

'Nay, that *must* be a mistake, sir! who, even in this extravagant and reckless country, could be found to pay such a price? One can fancy such a thing in a princess, with hundreds of thousands of income, but scarcely of any one else. How could such a thing be *used*, for instance?'

'Oh,' cried John Monson, 'to hide the blushes of the simpleton who had thrown away her money on it. I heard a story this very afternoon, of some person of the name of Halfacre's having failed yesterday, and whose daughter purchased even a higher-priced handkerchief than that the very same day.'

'His failure is not surprising, then,' put in Betts Shoreham. 'For myself, I do not think that I –'

'Well, *what* do you think, Mr. Shoreham?' asked Mrs. Monson, smiling, for she saw that Julia was too much mortified to speak, and who assumed more than half the blame of her own daughter's extravagance. 'You were about to favor us with some magnificent resolution.'

'I was about to utter an impertinence, I confess, ma'am, but recollected in time, that young men's protestations of what *they* would do by way of reforming the world, is not of half the importance to others that they so often fancy; so I shall spare you the infliction. Seventy-five dollars, Mademoiselle Hennequin, would be a high price for such a thing, even in Paris, I fancy.'

The answer was given in imperfect English, a circumstance that rendered the sweet round tones of the speaker very agreeable to the ear, and lent the charm of piquancy to what she said. I could not distinguish countenances from the drawer, but I fancied young Shoreham to be a handsome youth, the governess to be pale and slightly ugly, though very agreeable in manner, and Julia excessively embarrassed, but determined to defend her purchase, should it become necessary.

'Seventy-five dollars sounds like a high price, monsieur,' answered Mlle Hennequin; 'but the ladies of Paris do not grudge their gold for ornaments to decorate their persons.'

'Aye,' put in John Monson, 'but they are consistent. Now I'll engage this Mrs. Hundredacres, or Halfacre, or whatever her name may be, overlooked her own household work, kept no housekeeper, higgled about flour and butter, and lived half her time in her basement. Think of such a woman's giving her daughter a hundred-dollar pocket handkerchief.'

Now Mrs. Monson *did* keep a housekeeper; she was *not* a mere upper-servant in her own family, and Julia was gratified that, in this instance, her fastidious brother could not reproach *her* at least.

'Well, Jack, that is a queer reason of yours,' cried the father, 'for not indulging in a luxury; because the good woman is careful in some things, she is not to be a little extravagant in others. What do YOU say to such logic, Mr. Shoreham?'

'To own the truth, sir, I am much of Monson's way of thinking. It is as necessary to begin at the bottom in constructing a scheme of domestic refinement, as in building a house. Fitness is entitled to a place in every thing that relates to taste, at all events; and as a laced and embroidered pocket handkerchief is altogether for appearance, it becomes necessary that other things should be in keeping. If the ladies will excuse me, I will say that I never yet saw a woman in America, in a sufficiently high dress to justify such an appendage as that which Monson has just mentioned. The handkerchief ought not to cost more than the rest of the toilette.'

'It is true, Mr. Shoreham,' put in Julia, with vivacity, if not with spirit, 'that our women do not dress as women of rank sometimes dress in Europe; but, on the whole, I do not know that we are so much behind them in appearance.'

'Very far from it, my dear Miss Monson – as far as possible – I am the last man to decry my beautiful countrywomen, who are second to no others in appearance, certainly; if they do not dress as richly, it is because they do not need it. Mademoiselle Hennequin has no reason to deprecate comparisons – and – but – '

'Certainly,' answered the governess, when she found the young man hesitated about proceeding, 'certainly; I am not so bigoted, or so blind, as to wish to deny that the American ladies are very handsome – handsomer, as a whole, than those of my own country. It would be idle to deny it – so are those of England and Italy.'

'This is being very liberal, Mademoiselle Hennequin, and more than you are required to admit,' observed Mrs. Monson, in the kindest possible tone of voice, and I make no manner of doubt with a most benevolent smile, though I could not see her. 'Some of the most brilliantly beautiful women I have ever seen, have been French – perhaps the *most* brilliantly beautiful.'

'That is true, also, madame; but such is not the rule, I think. Both the English and Americans seem to me handsomer, as a whole, than my own countrywomen.' Now, nothing could be sweeter, or softer, or gentler, than the voice that made this great concession – for great it certainly was, as coming from a woman. It appeared to me that the admission, too, was more than commonly generous, from the circumstance that the governess was not particularly pretty in her own person. It is true, I had not yet seen her, but my mesmeritic impulses induced me to fancy as much.

'What say the *young* gentlemen to this?' asked Mr. Monson, laughing. 'This is a question not to be settled altogether by ladies, old or young.'

'Betts Shoreham has substantially told you what *he* thinks; and now I claim a right to give my opinion,' cried John Monson. 'Like Betts, I will not decry my countrywomen, but I shall protest against the doctrine of their having *all* the beauty in the world. By Jove! I have seen in *one* opera house at Rome more beautiful women than I ever saw together, before or since, in any other place. Broadway never equals the Corso[97] of a carnival.'

'This is not sticking to the subject,' observed Mrs. Monson. 'Pocket handkerchiefs and housekeepers are our themes, and not pretty women. Mademoiselle Hennequin, you are French enough, I am sure, to like more sugar in your tea.'

This changed the subject, which became a desultory discourse on the news of the day. I could not understand half that was said, laboring under the disadvantage of being shut up in a close drawer, on another floor; and that, too, with six dozen of chattering French gloves lying within a foot of me. Still I saw plainly enough that Mlle Hennequin, notwithstanding she was a governess, was a favorite in the family; and, I may add, out of it also – Betts Shoreham being no sort of a connection of the Monsons. I thought, moreover, that I discovered signs of cross-purposes, as between the young people, though I think a pocket handkerchief subject to those general laws, concerning secrets, that are recognized among all honorable persons. Not having been actually present on this occasion, should I proceed to relate *all* that passed, or that I fancied passed, it would be degrading myself to the level of those newspapers that are in the habit of retailing private conversations, and which, like most small dealers in such things, never retail fairly.

I saw no more of my mistress for a week. I have reason to think that she had determined never to use me; but female resolutions, in matters of dress, are not of the most inflexible nature. There was a certain Mrs. Leamington, in New York, who gave a great ball about this time, and being in the same set as the Monsons, the family was invited as a matter of course. It would have surpassed the powers of self-denial to keep me in the background on such an occasion; and Julia, having first cleared the way by owning her folly to a very indulgent father, and a very tormenting brother, determined nobly to bring me out, let the effect on Betts Shoreham be what it might. As the father had no female friends to trouble him, he was asked to join the Monsons – the intimacy fully warranting the step.

Julia never looked more lovely than she did that night. She anticipated much pleasure, and her smiles were in proportion to her anticipations. When all was ready, she took me from the drawer, let a single drop of lavender fall in my bosom, and tripped down stairs toward the drawing room; Betts Shoreham and Mlle Hennequin were together, and, for a novelty, alone. I say, for a novelty, because the governess had few opportunities to see anyone without the presence of a third person, and because her habits, as an unmarried and well-educated French woman, indisposed her to tête-à-têtes with the other sex. My mistress was lynx-eyed in all that related to Betts Shoreham and the governess. A single glance told her that their recent conversation had been more than usually interesting; nor could I help seeing it myself – the face of the governess being red, or in that condition that, were she aught but a governess, would be called suffused with blushes. Julia felt uncomfortable – she felt herself to be *de trop*;[98] and making an incoherent excuse, she had scarcely taken a seat on a sofa, before she arose, left the room, and ran up stairs again. In doing so, however, the poor girl left me inadvertently on the sofa she had so suddenly quitted herself.

Betts Shoreham manifested no concern at this movement, though Mlle Hennequin precipitately changed her seat, which had been quite near – approximately near, as one might say – to the chair occupied by the gentleman. This new evolution placed the governess close at my side. Now whatever might have been the subject of discourse between these two young persons – for Mlle Hennequin was quite as youthful as my mistress, let her beauty be as it might – it was not continued in my presence; on the contrary, the young lady turned her eyes on me, instead of looking at her companion, and then she raised me in her hand, and commenced a critical examination of my person.

'That is a very beautiful handkerchief, Mademoiselle Hennequin,' said Betts Shoreham, making the remark an excuse for following the young lady to the sofa. 'Had we heard of its existence, our remarks the other night, on such a luxury, might have been more guarded.'

No answer was given. The governess gazed on me intently, and tears began to course down her cheeks, notwithstanding it was evident she wished to conceal them. Ashamed of her weakness, she endeavored to smile them away, and to appear cheerful.

'What is there in that pocket handkerchief, dear Mademoiselle Hennequin,' asked Betts Shoreham, who had a pernicious habit of calling young ladies with whom he was on terms of tolerable intimacy, 'dear,' – a habit that sometimes misled persons as to the degree of interest he felt in his companions – 'what *can* there be in that pocket handkerchief to excite tears from a mind and a heart like yours?'

'My mind and heart, Mr. Shoreham, are not as faultless, perhaps, as your goodness would make them out to be. *Envy* is a very natural feeling for a woman in matters of dress, they say; and, certainly, I am not the owner of so beautiful a pocket handkerchief – pardon me,

Mr. Shoreham; I cannot command myself, and must be guilty of the rudeness of leaving you alone, if – '

Mademoiselle Hennequin uttered no more, but rushed from the room, with an impetuosity of manner and feeling that I have often had occasion to remark in young French women. As a matter of course, I was left alone with Betts Shoreham.

I shall conceal nothing that ought to be told. Betts Shoreham, not-withstanding her dependent situation, and his own better fortunes, loved the governess, and the governess loved Betts Shoreham. These were facts that I discovered at a later day, though I began to suspect the truth from that moment. Neither, however, knew of the other's passion, though each hoped as an innocent and youthful love will hope, and each trembled as each hoped. Nothing explicit had been said that evening; but much, very much, in the way of sympathy and feeling had been revealed, and but for the inopportune entrance of Julia and myself, all might have been told.

15

There is no moment in the life of man when he is so keenly sensitive on the subject of the perfection of his mistress, as that in which he com-pletely admits her power. All his jealousy is actively alive to the smallest shade of fault, although his feelings so much indispose him to see any blemish. Betts Shoreham felt an unpleasant pang, even – yes, it amounted to a pang – for in a few moments he would have offered his hand – and men cannot receive any drawback with indifference at such an instant – he felt an unpleasant pang, then, as the idea crossed his mind that Mlle Hennequin could be so violently affected by a feeling as unworthy as that of envy. He had passed several years abroad, and had got the common notion about the selfishness of the French, and more particularly their women, and his prejudices took the alarm. But his love was much the strongest, and soon looked down the distrust, however reasonable, under the circumstances, the latter might have appeared to a disinterested and cool-headed observer. He had seen so much meek and pure-spirited self-denial, so much high principle in the conduct of Mlle Hennequin, during an intimacy that had now lasted six months, that no passing feeling of doubt, like the one just felt, could unsettle the confidence created by her virtues. I know it may take more credit than belongs to most pocket hand-kerchiefs, to maintain the problem of the virtues of a French governess – a class of unfortunate persons that seem doomed to condemnation by all the sages of our modern imaginative literature. An English governess, or even an American governess, if, indeed, there be such a being in nature, may be everything that is respectable, and prudent, and wise, and good; but the French governess has a sort of ex officio moral taint about her, which throws her without the pale of literary charities. Nevertheless, one or two of the most excellent women I have ever known have been French governesses, though I do not choose to reveal what this particular indivi-dual of the class turned out to be in the end, until the moment for the denouement of her character shall regularly arrive.

There was not much time for Betts Shoreham to philosophize, and speculate on female caprices and motives, John Monson making his appearance in as high evening dress as well comported with what is called 'republican simplicity.' John was a fine-looking fellow, six feet and an inch, with large whiskers, a bushy head of hair, and particularly white teeth. His friend was two inches shorter, of much less showy appearance, but of a more intellectual countenance, and of juster proportions. Most persons, at first sight, would praise John Monson's person and face, but all would feel the superiority of Betts Shoreham's, on an acquaintance. The smile of the latter, in particular, was as winning and amiable as that of a girl. It was that smile, on the one hand, and his active, never dormant sympathy for her situation, on the other, which, united, had made such an inroad on the young governess's affections.

'It's deuced cold, Betts,' said John, as he came near the fire; 'this delightful country of ours has some confounded hard winters. I wonder if it be patriotic to say, *our* winters?'

'It's all common property, Monson – but, what have become of your sister and Mademoiselle Hennequin? They were both here a minute since, and have vanished like –'

'What? – ghosts! – no, you dare not call them *that*, lest their spirits take it in dudgeon. Julie is no ghost, though she is sometimes so delicate and ethereal, and as for Henny – '

'Who?' exclaimed Betts, doubting if his ears were true.

'Henny, Tote and Moll's governess. Whom do you think I could mean, else? I always call her Henny, en famille, and I look upon you as almost one of us since our travels.'

'I'm sure I can scarcely be grateful enough, my dear fellow – but, you do not call her so to her face?'

'Why – no – perhaps not exactly in her very teeth – and beautiful teeth she has, Betts – Julie's won't compare with them.'

'Miss Monson has fine teeth, notwithstanding. Perhaps Mademoiselle Hennequin –'

'Yes, Henny has the best teeth of any girl I know. They are none of your pearls – some pearls are yellowish, you know – but they are teeth; just what ought to be in a handsome girl's mouth. I have no objection to pearls in a necklace, or in the pockets, but *teeth* are what are wanted in a mouth, and Henny has just the finest set I know of.'

Betts Shoreham fidgeted at the 'Henny,' and he had the weakness, at the moment, to wish the young governess were not in a situation to be spoken of so unceremoniously. He had not time to express this feeling, before John Monson got a glimpse of me, and had me under examination beneath the light of a very powerful lamp. I declare that, knowing his aversion to our species, I felt a glow in all my system at the liberties he was taking.

'What have we here?' exclaimed John Monson, in surprise; 'has Miss Flowergarden made a call, and is this her card?'

'I believe that pocket handkerchief belongs to your sister,' answered Betts, drily, 'if that be what you mean.'

'Jule! well, I am sorry to hear it. I did hope that no sister of *mine* would run into any such foolish extravagance – do you own it, Jule?' who entered the room at that instant – 'is this bit of a rag yours, or is it not more likely to be Henny's?'

'Bit of a rag!' cried the sister, snatching me dexterously out of the spoiler's hands; 'and "Henny," too! This is not a bit of a rag, sir, but a very pretty pocket handkerchief, and you must very well know that Mademoiselle Hennequin is not likely to be the owner of any thing as costly.'

'And what did it cost, pray? At least tell me *that*, if nothing else.'

'I shall not gratify your curiosity, sir – a lady's wardrobe is not to be dissected in this manner.'

'Pray, sir, may I ask,' Mr. Monson now coming in, 'did you pay for Jule's handkerchief? Hang me, if I ever saw a more vulgar thing in my life.'

'The opinion is not likely to induce me to say yes,' answered the father, half-laughing, and yet half-angry at his son's making such allusions before Betts – 'never mind him, my dear; the handkerchief is not half as expensive as his own cigars.'

'It shall be as thoroughly smoked, nevertheless,' rejoined John, who was as near being spoilt, and escaping, as was at all necessary. 'Ah, Julie, Julie, I'm ashamed of thee.'

This was an inauspicious commencement for an evening from which so much happiness had been anticipated, but Mrs. Monson coming down, and the carriages driving to the door, Mlle Hennequin was summoned, and the whole party left the house.

As a matter of course, it was a little out of the common way that the governess was asked to make one, in the invitations given to the Monsons. But Mlle Hennequin was a person of such perfect *bon ton*,[99] had so thoroughly the manners of a lady, and was generally reputed so accomplished, that most of the friends of the family felt themselves bound to notice her. There was another reason, too, which justice requires I should relate, though it is not so creditable to the young lady, as those already given. From some quarter, or other, a rumor had got abroad that Miss Monson's governess was of a noble family, a circumstance that I soon discovered had great influence in New York, doubtless by way of expiation for the rigid democratical notions that so universally pervade its society. And here I may remark, *en passant*,[100] that while nothing is considered so disreputable in America as to be 'aristocratic,' a word of very extensive signification, as it embraces the tastes, the opinions, the habits, the virtues, and sometimes the religion of the offending party – on the other hand, nothing is so certain to attract attention as nobility. How many poor Poles have I seen dragged about and made lions of, merely because they were reputed noble, though the distinction in that country is pretty much the same as that which exists in one portion of this great republic, where one half the population is white, and the other black, the former making the noble, and the latter the serf.

'What an exceedingly aristocratic pocket handkerchief Miss Monson has this evening,' observed Mrs. G. to Mr. W., as we passed into Mrs. Leamington's rooms, that evening; 'I don't know when I've seen anything so aristocratic in society.'

'The Monsons are very aristocratic in all things; I understand they dine at six.'

'Yes,' put in Miss F., 'and use finger bowls every day.'

'How aristocratic!'

'Very – they even say that since they have come back from Europe, the last time, matters are pushed further than ever. The ladies insist on kneeling at prayers, instead of inclining, like all the rest of the world.'

'Did one ever hear of any thing so aristocratic!'

'They *do* say, but I will not vouch for its truth, that Mr. and Mrs. Monson insist on all their children calling them "father" and "mother," instead of "pa" and "ma."'

'Why, Mr. W., that is downright monarchical, is it not?'

'It's difficult to say what is, and what is not monarchical, nowadays; though I think one is pretty safe in pronouncing it anti-republican.'

'It is patriarchal, rather,' observed a wit, who belonged to the group.

Into this 'aristocratical' *set* I was now regularly introduced. Many longing and curious eyes were drawn toward me, though the company in this house was generally too well-bred to criticize articles of dress very closely. Still, in every country, aristocracy, monarchy, or democracy, there are privileged classes, and in all companies privileged persons. One of the latter took the liberty of asking Julia to leave me in her keeping, while the other danced, and I was thus temporarily transferred to a circle, in which several other pocket handkerchiefs had been collected, with a view to compare our several merits and demerits. The reader will judge of my surprise, when, the examination being ended, and the judgment being rendered altogether in my favor, I found myself familiarly addressed by the name that I bore in the family circle, or, as No. 7; for pocket handkerchiefs never speak to each other except on the principle of decimals. It was No. 12, or my relative of the extreme *côté gauche*, who had strangely enough found his way into this very room, and was now lying cheek by jowl with me again, in old Mrs. Eyelet's lap. Family affection made us glad to meet, and we had a hundred questions to put to each other in a breath.

No. 12 had commenced life a violent republican, and this simply because he read nothing but republican newspapers, a sufficiently simple reason, as all know who have heard both sides of any question. Shortly after I was purchased by poor, dear Adrienne, a young American traveler had stepped into the *magasin*, and with the recklessness that distinguishes the expenditures of his countrymen, swept off half a dozen of the family at one purchase. Accident gave him the liberal end of the piece, a circumstance to which he never would have assented had he known the fact, for being an attaché of the legation of his own country, he was ex officio aristocratic. My brother amused me exceedingly with his account of the indignation he felt at finding himself in a very hotbed of monarchical opinions, in the set at the American legation. What rendered these *diplomates*[101] so much the more aristocratic, was the novelty of the thing, scarcely one of them having been accustomed to society at home. After passing a few months in such company, my brother's boss, who was a mere traveling diplomatist, came home and began to run a brilliant career in the circles of New York, on the faith of a European reputation. Alas! there is in pocket-handkerchief nature a disposition to act by contraries. The 'more you call, the more I won't come' principle was active in poor No. 12's mind, and he had not been a month in New York society, before he came out an ultra monarchist. New York society has more than one of these sudden political conversions to answer for. It is such a thorough development of the democratic principle that the faith of few believers is found strong enough to withstand it. Everybody knows how much a prospect varies by position. Thus, you shall stand on the aristocratic side of a room filled with company, and every thing will present a vulgar and democratic appearance; or, vice versa, you shall occupy a place among the hoi polloi, and all is aristocratic, exclusive, and offensive. So it had proved with my unfortunate kinsman. All his notions had changed; instead of finding the perfection he had preached and extolled so long, he found nothing to admire, and every thing to condemn. In a word, never was a pocket handkerchief so miserable, and that, too, on grounds so philosophical and profound, met with, on its entrance into active life. I do believe, if my brother could have got back to France, he would have written a book on America, which, while it overlooked many vices and foibles that deserve to be cut up without mercy, would have thrown even de Tocqueville[102] into the shade in the way of political blunders. But I forbear, this latter writer being unanswerable among those neophytes who having never thought of their own system, unless as Englishmen, are overwhelmed with admiration at finding any thing of another character advanced about it. At least, such are the sentiments entertained by a very high-priced pocket handkerchief.

Mademoiselle Hennequin, I took occasion to remark, occupied much of the attention of Betts Shoreham, at Mrs. Leamington's ball. They understood each other perfectly, though the young man could not get over the feeling created by the governess's manner when she first met with me. Throughout the evening, indeed, her eye seemed studiously averted from me, as if she struggled to suppress certain sentiments or sensations, that she was unwilling to betray. Now, these sentiments, if sentiments they were, or sensations, as they were beyond all dispute, might be envy – repinings at another's better fortunes – or they might be excited by philosophical and commendable reflections touching those follies that so often lead the young and thoughtless into extravagance. Betts tried hard to believe them the last, though, in his inmost heart, he would a thousand times rather that the woman he loved should smile on a weakness of this sort, in a girl of her own age, than that she should show herself to be prematurely wise, if it was wisdom purchased at the expense of the light-heartedness and sympathies of her years and sex. On a diminished scale, I had awakened in his bosom some such uneasy distrust as the pocket handkerchief of Desdemona is known to have aroused in that of the Moor.[103]

Nor can I say that Julia Monson enjoyed herself as much as she had anticipated. Love she did not Betts Shoreham; for that was a passion her temperament and training induced her to wait for some pretty unequivocal demonstrations on the part of the gentleman before she yielded to it; but she *liked* him vastly, and nothing would have been easier than to have blown this smoldering preference into a flame. She was too young, and, to say the truth, too natural and uncalculating, to be always remembering that Betts owned a good old-fashioned landed estate that was said to produce twenty, and which did actually produce 11,000 a year, net; and that his house in the country was generally said to be one of the very best in the state. For all this she cared absolutely nothing, or nothing worth mentioning. There were enough young men of as good estates, and there were a vast many of no estates at all, ready and willing to take their chances in the 'cutting up' of 'old Monson,' but there were few who were as agreeable, as well mannered, as handsome, or who had seen as much of the world, as Betts Shoreham. Of course, she had never fancied the young man in love with herself, but, previously to the impression she had quite recently imbibed of his attachment to her mother's governess, she had been accustomed to think such a thing *might* come to pass, and that she should not be sorry if it did.

I very well understand this is not the fashionable, or possibly the polite way of describing those incipient sentiments that form the germ of love in the virgin affections of young ladies, and that a skillful and refined poet would use very different language on the occasion; but I began this history to represent things as they are, and such is the manner in which 'Love's Young Dream'[104] appears to a pocket handkerchief.

Among other things that were unpleasant, Miss Monson was compelled to overhear sundry remarks of Betts's devotion to the governess, as she stood in the dance, some of which reached me, also.

'Who is the lady to whom Mr. Shoreham is so *dévoué*[105] this evening?' asked Miss N. of Miss T. "Tis quite a new face, and, if one might be so presuming, quite a new manner.'

'That is Mademoiselle Henny, the governess of Mrs. Monson's children, my dear. They say she is all accomplishments, and quite a miracle of propriety. It is also rumored that she is, some way, a very distinguished person, reduced by those horrid revolutions of which they have so many in Europe.'

'Noble, I dare say!'

'Oh! that at least. Some persons affirm that she is semi-*royal*. The country is full of broken-down royalty and nobility. Do you think she has an aristocratic air?'

'Not in the least – her ears are too small.'

'Why, my dear, that is the very symbol of nobility! When my Aunt Harding was in Naples, she knew the Duke of Montecarbana, intimately; and she says he had the smallest ears she ever beheld on a human being. The Montecarbanas are a family as old as the ruins of Paestum,[106] they say.'

'Well, to my notion, nobility and teaching little girls French and Italian, and their *gammes*,[107] have very little in common. I had thought Mr. Shoreham an admirer of Miss Monson's.'

Now, unfortunately, my mistress overheard this remark. Her feelings were just in that agitated state to take the alarm, and she determined to flirt with a young man of the name of Thurston, with a view to awaken Betts's jealousy, if he had any, and to give vent to her own spleen. This Tom Thurston was one of those tall, good-looking young fellows who come from nobody knows where, get into society nobody knows how, and live on nobody knows what. It was pretty generally understood that he was on the lookout for a rich wife, and encouragement from Julia Monson was not likely to be disregarded by such a person. To own the truth, my mistress carried matters much too far – so far, indeed, as to attract attention from everybody but those most concerned, viz. her own mother and Betts Shoreham. Although elderly ladies play cards very little, just now, in American society, or, indeed, in any other, they have their inducements for rendering the well-known office of matron at a ball, a mere sinecure. Mrs. Monson, too, was an indulgent mother, and seldom saw anything very wrong in her own children. Julia, in the main, had sufficient *retenue*, and a suspicion of her want of discretion on this point was one of the last things that would cross the fond parent's mind at Mrs. Leamington's ball. Others, however, were less confiding.

'Your daughter is in *high spirits* tonight,' observed a single lady of a certain age, who was sitting near Mrs. Monson; 'I do not remember to have ever seen her so *gay*.'

'Yes, dear girl, she IS happy,' – poor Julia was any thing but *that*, just then – 'but youth is the time for happiness, if it is ever to come in this life.'

'Is Miss Monson addicted to such *very* high spirits?' continued one, who was resolute to torment, and vexed that the mother could not be sufficiently alarmed to look around.

'Always – when in agreeable company. I think it a great happiness, ma'am, to possess good spirits.'

'No doubt – yet one needn't be always fifteen, as Lady Wortley Montagu[108] said,' muttered the other, giving up the point, and changing her seat, in order that she might speak her mind more freely into the ear of a congenial spirit.

Half an hour later we were all in the carriages, again, on our way home; all, but Betts Shoreham, I should say, for having seen the ladies cloaked, he had taken his leave at Mrs. Leamington's door, as uncertain as ever whether or not to impute envy to a being who, in all other respects, seemed to him to be faultless. He had to retire to an uneasy pillow, undetermined whether to pursue his original intention of making the poor friendless French girl independent, by an offer of his hand, or whether to decide that her amiable and gentle qualities were all seeming, and that she was not what she appeared to be. Betts Shoreham owed his distrust to national prejudice, and well was he paid for entertaining so vile a companion. Had Mlle Hennequin been an American girl, he would not have thought a second time of the emotion she had betrayed in regarding my beauties; but he had been taught to believe all French women managing and hypocritical, a notion that the experience of a young man in Paris would not be very likely to destroy.

'Well,' cried John Monson, as the carriage drew from Mrs. Leamington's door, 'this is the last ball I shall go to in New York;' which declaration he repeated twenty times that season, and as often broke.

'What is the matter now, Jack?' demanded the father. 'I found it very pleasant – six or seven of us old fellows made a very agreeable evening of it.'

'Yes, I dare say, sir; but you were not compelled to dance in a room eighteen by twenty-four, with a hundred people treading on your toes, or brushing their heads in your face.'

'Jack can find no room for dancing since the great ball of the *Salle de l'Opéra*,[109] at Paris,' observed the mother smiling. 'I hope you enjoyed yourself better, Julia?'

My mistress started; then she answered with a sort of hysterical glee – 'Oh! I have found the evening delightful, ma'am. I could have remained two hours longer.'

'And you, Mademoiselle Hennequin; I hope you, too, were agreeably entertained?'

The governess answered meekly, and with a slight tremor in her voice.

'Certainly, madame,' she said, 'I have enjoyed myself; though dancing always seems an amusement I have no right to share in.'

There was some little embarrassment, and I could perceive an impulse in Julia to press nearer to her rival, as if impelled by a generous wish to manifest her sympathy. But Tom's protest soon silenced every thing else, and we alighted, and soon went to rest.

The next morning Julia sent for me down to be exhibited to one or two friends, my fame having spread in consequence of my late appearance. I was praised, kissed, called a pretty dear, and extolled like a spoiled child, though Miss W. did not fail to carry the intelligence, far and near, that Miss Monson's much-talked-of pocket handkerchief was nothing after all but the *thing* Miss Halfacre had brought out the night of the day her father had stopped payment. Some even began to nickname me the insolvent pocket handkerchief.

I thought Julia sad, after her friends had all left her. I lay neglected on a sofa, and the pretty girl's brow became thoughtful. Of a sudden she was aroused from a brown study – reflective mood, perhaps, would be a more select phrase – by the unexpected appearance of young Thurston. There was a sort of 'Ah! have I caught you alone?' expression about this adventurer's eye, even while he was making his bow, that struck me. I looked for great events, nor was I altogether disappointed. In one minute he was seated at Julia's side, on the same sofa, and within two feet of her; in two more he had brought in play his usual tricks of flattery. My mistress listened languidly, and yet not altogether without interest. She was piqued at Betts Shoreham's indifference, had known her present admirer several months, if dancing in the same set can be called *knowing*, and had never been made love to before, at least in a manner so direct and unequivocal. The young man had tact enough to discover that he had an advantage, and fearful that some one might come in and interrupt the tête-à-tête, he magnanimously resolved to throw all on a single cast, and come to the point at once.

'I think, Miss Monson,' he continued, after a very beautiful specimen of rigmarole in the way of love-making, a rigmarole that might have very fairly figured in an editor's law and logic, after he had been beaten in a libel suit, 'I think, Miss Monson, you cannot have overlooked the *very* particular attentions I have endeavored to pay you, ever since I have been so fortunate as to have made your acquaintance?'

'I! – Upon my word, Mr. Thurston, I am not at all conscious of having been the object of any such attentions!'

'No? – That is ever the way with the innocent and single-minded! This is what we sincere and diffident men have to contend with in affairs of the heart. Our bosoms may be torn with ten thousand distracting cares, and yet the modesty of a truly virtuous female heart shall be so absorbed in its own placid serenity as to be indifferent to the pangs it is unconsciously inflicting!'

'Mr. Thurston, your language is strong – and – a little – a little unintelligible.'

'I dare say – ma'am – I never expect to be intelligible again. When the "heart is oppressed with unutterable anguish, condemned to conceal that passion which is at once the torment and delight of life" – when "his lip, the ruby harbinger of joy, lies pale and cold, the miserable appendage of a mang–" that is, Miss Monson, I mean to say, when all our faculties are engrossed by one dear object we are often incoherent and mysterious, as a matter of course.'

Tom Thurston came very near wrecking himself on the quicksands of the romantic school. He had begun to quote from a speech delivered by Gouverneur Morris, on the right of deposit at New Orleans,[110] and which he had spoken at college, and was near getting into a part of the subject that might not have been so apposite, but retreated in time. By way of climax, the lover laid his hand on me, and raised me to his eyes in an abstracted manner, as if unconscious of what he was doing, and wanted to brush away a tear.

'What a confounded rich old fellow the father must be,' thought Tom, 'to give her such pocket handkerchiefs!'

I felt like a wren that escapes from the hawk when the rogue laid me down.

Alas! Poor Julia was the dupe of all this acting. Totally unpracticed herself, abandoned by the usages of the society in which she had been educated very much to the artifices of any fortune-hunter, and vexed with Betts Shoreham, she was in the worst possible frame of mind to resist such eloquence and love. She had seen Tom at all the balls in the best houses, found no fault with his exterior and manners, both of which were fashionable and showy, and now discovered that he had a most sympathetic heart, over which, unknown to herself, she had obtained a very unlimited control.

'You do not answer me, Miss Monson,' continued Tom peeping out at one side of me, for I was still at his eyes – 'you do not answer me, cruel, inexorable girl!'

'What *would* you have me say, Mr. Thurston?'

'Say *yes*, dearest, loveliest, most perfect being of the whole human family.'

'*Yes*, then; if that will relieve your mind, it is a relief very easily bestowed.'

Now, Tom Thurston was as skilled in a fortune-hunter's wiles as Napoleon was in military strategy. He saw he had obtained an immense advantage for the future, and he forbore to press the matter any further at the moment. The 'yes' had been uttered more in pleasantry than with any other feeling, but, by holding it in reserve, presuming on it gradually, and using it in a crisis, it might be worth – 'let me see,' calculated Tom, as he went whistling down Broadway, 'that "yes" may be made to yield at least a cool $100,000. There are John, this girl, and two little ones. Old Monson is worth every dollar of $700,000 – none of your skyrockets, but a known, old fortune, in substantial houses and lands – let us suppose the old woman outlive him, and that she gets her full thirds; *that* will leave $466,660. Perhaps John may get a couple of hundred thousand, and even *then* each of the girls will have $88,888. If one of the little things should happen to die, and there's lots of scarlet fever about, why that would fetch it up at once to a round hundred thousand. I don't think the old woman would be likely to marry again at her time of life. One mustn't calculate too confidently on *that*, however, as I would have her myself for half of *such* thirds.'

16

For a week nothing material transpired. All that time I lay in the drawer, gaining a knowledge of what passed, in the best manner I could. Betts Shoreham was a constant visitor at the house, and Tom Thurston made his appearance with a degree of punctuality that began to attract notice, among the inmates of the house on the opposite side of the street. All this time, however, Tom treated Julia with the greatest respect, and even distance, turning more of his attention toward Mrs. Monson. He acted in this manner, because he thought he had secured a sufficient lien on the young lady, by means of her 'yes,' and knew how important it was for one who could show none of the usual inducements for consent, to the parents, to obtain the goodwill of the 'old lady.'

At the end of the week, Mrs. Monson opened her house to receive the world. As a matter of course, I was brought out on this occasion. Now, Betts Shoreham and Mlle Hennequin had made great progress toward an understanding in the course of this week, though the lady becoming more and more conscious of the interest she had created in the heart of the gentleman, her own conduct got to be cautious and reserved. At length, Betts actually carried matters so far as to write a letter, which was as much to the point as a man could very well come. In a word, he offered his hand to the excellent young French woman, assuring her, in very passionate and suitable terms, that she had been mistress of his affections ever since the first month of their acquaintance. In this letter, he implored her not to be so cruel as to deny him an interview, and there were a few exceedingly pretty reproaches, touching her recent coy and reserved deportment.

Mademoiselle Hennequin was obliged to read this letter in Julia's room, and she took such a position to do it as exposed every line to my impertinent gaze, as I lay on the bed, among the other finery that was got out for the evening. Mrs. Monson was present, and she had summoned the governess, in order to consult her on the subject of some of the ornaments of the supper table. Fortunately, both Julia and her mother were too much engaged to perceive the tears that rolled down the cheeks of the poor stranger, as she read the honest declaration of a fervid and manly love, nor did either detect the manner in which the letter was pressed to Mlle Hennequin's heart, when she had done reading it the second time.

Just at this instant a servant came to announce Mr. Shoreham's presence in the 'breakfast room.' This was a retired and little-frequented part of the house at that hour, Betts having been shown into it in consequence of the preparations that were going on in the proper reception rooms.

'Julia, my dear, you will have to go below – although it is at a most inconvenient moment.'

'No, mother – let Mr. Betts Shoreham time his visits better – George, say that the ladies are *engaged.*'

'That will not do,' interrupted the mother, in some concern – 'we are too intimate for such an excuse – would *you*, Mademoiselle Hennequin, have the goodness to see Mr. Shoreham for a few minutes – you must come into our American customs sooner or later, and this may be a favorable moment to commence.'

Mrs. Monson laughed pleasantly as she made this request, and her kindness and delicacy to the governess were too marked and unremitted to permit the latter to think of hesitating. She had laid her own handkerchief down at my side, to read the letter, but feeling the necessity of drying her eyes, she caught me up by mistake, smiled her assent, and left the apartment.

Mademoiselle Hennequin did not venture below, until she had gone into her own room. Here she wept freely for a minute or two, and then she bathed her eyes in cold water, and used the napkin in drying them. Owing to this circumstance, I was fortunately a witness of all that passed in her interview with her lover.

The instant Betts Shoreham saw that he was to have an interview with the charming French girl, instead of with Julia Monson, his countenance brightened; and, as if supposing the circumstance proof of his success, he seized the governess's hand, and carried it to his lips in a very carnivorous fashion. The lady, however, succeeded in retaining her hand, if she did not positively preserve it from being devoured.

'A thousand, thousand thanks, dearest Mademoiselle Hennequin,' said Betts, in an incoherent, half-sane manner; 'you have read my letter, and I may interpret this interview favorably. I meant to have told all to

Mrs. Monson, had *she* come down, and asked her kind interference – but it is much, much better as it is.'

'You will do well, monsieur, not to speak to Madame Monson on the subject at all,' answered Mademoiselle Hennequin, with an expression of countenance that I found quite inexplicable; since it was not happy, nor was it altogether the reverse. 'This must be our last meeting, and it were better that no one knew any thing of its nature.'

'Then my vanity – my hopes have misled me, and I have no interest in your feelings!'

'I do not say *that*, monsieur; oh! *non – non* – I am far from saying as much as *that*' – poor girl, her face declared a hundred times more than her tongue that she was sincere – 'I do not – *cannot* say I have no interest in one who so generously overlooks my poverty, my utter destitution of all worldly greatness, and offers to share with me his fortune and his honorable position –'

'This is not what I ask – what I had hoped to earn – gratitude is not love.'

'Gratitude easily becomes love in a woman's heart' – answered the dear creature, with a smile and a look that Betts would have been a mere dolt not to have comprehended – 'and it is my duty to take care that MY gratitude does not entertain this weakness.'

'Mademoiselle Hennequin, for mercy's sake, be as frank and simple as I know your nature prompts – *do* you, *can* you love me?'

Of course such a direct question, put in a very categorical way, caused the questioned to blush, if it did not induce her to smile. The first she did in a very pretty and engaging manner, though I thought she hesitated about indulging in the last.

'Why should I say "yes," when it can lead to no good result?'

'Then destroy all hope at once, and say *no*.'

'That would be to give you – to give us both unnecessary pain. Besides, it might not be strictly true – I *could* love – Oh! No one can tell how my heart *could* love where it was right and proper.'

After this, I suppose it is unnecessary for me to say, that Betts soon brought the category of possibilities into one of certainty. To own the truth, he carried everything by his impetuosity, reducing the governess to own that what she admitted she *could* do so well, she had already done in a very complete and thorough manner. I enjoyed this scene excessively, nor was it over in a minute. Mademoiselle Hennequin used me several times to wipe away tears, and it is strong proof how much both parties were thinking of other matters, that neither discovered who was present at so interesting a tête-à-tête.

At length came the denouement. After confessing how much she loved Betts, how happy she would be could she be his slave all the days of her life, how miserable she was in knowing that he had placed his affections on *her*, and how much more miserable she should be had she learned he had *not*, Mlle Hennequin almost annihilated the young man by declaring that it was utterly impossible for her to consent to become his wife. The reason was the difference in fortune, and the impossibility that she should take advantage of his passion to lead him into a connection that he might afterwards regret. Against this decision, Betts reasoned warmly, but seriously, in vain. Had Mlle Hennequin been an American, instead of a French, girl, her feelings would not have been so sensitive on this point, for, in this great republic, everybody but the fortune-hunters, an exceedingly contemptible class, considers a match without money quite as much a matter of course as a match with. But, the governess had been educated under a different system, and it struck her imagination as very proper that she should make both herself and her lover miserable, because he had 200,000 dollars, and she had not as many hundreds. All this strangely conflicted with Betts' preconceived opinion of a French woman's selfishness, and, while he was disposed to believe his adored perfection, he almost feared it was a trick. Of such contradictory materials is the human mind composed!

At length the eyes of Betts fell on me, who was still in the hand of Mlle Hennequin, and had several times been applied to her eyes unheeded. It was evident I revived unpleasant recollections, and the young man could not avoid letting an expression escape him, that sufficiently betrayed his feelings.

'This handkerchief!' exclaimed the young governess – 'Ah! it is that of Mademoiselle Julie, which I must have taken by mistake. But, why should this handkerchief awaken any feeling in you, monsieur? You are not about to enact the Moor, in your days of wooing?'[111]

This was said sweetly, and withal a little archly, for the poor girl was glad to turn the conversation from its harassing and painful points; but Betts was in no humor for pleasantry, and he spoke out in a way to give his mistress some clue to his thoughts.

'That cursed handkerchief' – it is really indecent in young men to use such improper language, but they little heed what they say when strongly excited – 'that cursed handkerchief has given me as much pain, as it appears also to have given you. I wish I knew the real secret of its connection with your feelings; for I confess, like that of Desdemona's, it has excited distrust, though for a very different cause.'

The cheeks of Mlle Hennequin were pale, and her brow thoughtful. Still, she had a sweet smile for Betts; and, though ignorant of the nature of his suspicions, which she would have scarcely pardoned, it was her strongest wish to leave no darker cloud between them than the one she felt it her duty to place there herself. She answered, therefore, frankly and simply, though not without betraying strong emotion as she proceeded.

'This handkerchief is well known to me,' answered the young French woman; 'it revives the recollections of some of the most painful scenes of a life that has never seen much sunshine. You have heard me speak of a grandmother, Mr. Shoreham, who took care of my childhood, and who died in my arms. That handkerchief, I worked for her support in her last illness, and this lace – yes, this beautiful lace was a part of that beloved grandmother's bridal trousseau. I put it where you see it, to enhance the value of my labors.'

'I *see* it all!' exclaimed the repentant Betts – '*feel* it all, dearest, dearest Mademoiselle Hennequin; and I hope this exquisite work, this refined taste brought all the comfort and reward you had a right to anticipate.'

A shade of anguish crossed the face of Adrienne – for it was no other – as she gazed at me, and recalled all the scenes of her sufferings and distress. Then I knew her again, for time and a poor memory, with some development of person, had caused me to forget the appearance of the lovely creature who may be said to have made me what I am; but one glance at her, with that expression of intense suffering on her countenance, renewed all my earlier impressions.

'I received as much as I merited, perhaps,' returned the meek-minded girl – for she was proud only in insisting on what she fancied right – 'and enough to give my venerated parent Christian burial. They were days of want and sorrow that succeeded, during which, Betts, I toiled for bread like an Eastern slave, the trodden-on and abused hireling of a selfish milliner. Accident at length placed me in a family as a governess. This family happened to be acquainted with Madame Monson, and an offer that was brilliant to me, in my circumstances, brought me to America. You see by all this how unfit I am to be your wife, monsieur. You would blush to have it said you had married a French milliner!'

'But you are not a milliner, in that sense, dearest Adrienne – for you must suffer me to call you by that name – you are a lady reduced by revolutions and misfortunes. The name of Hennequin I know is respectable, and what care I for money, when so much worth is to be found on your side of the scale. Money would only oppress me, under such circumstances.'

'Your generosity almost overcomes my scruples, but it may not be. The name to which I am entitled is certainly not one to be ashamed of – it is far more illustrious than that of Hennequin, respectable as is the last; but of what account is a *name* to one in my condition!'

'And your family name is not Hennequin?' asked the lover, anxiously.

'It is not. My poor grandmother assumed the name of Hennequin when we went last to Paris, under an apprehension that the guillotine might follow the revolution of July, as it had followed that of '89. This name she enjoined it on me to keep, and I have never thought it prudent to change it. I am of the family of de la Rocheaimard.'

The exclamation that burst from the lips of Betts Shoreham betokened both surprise and delight. He made Adrienne repeat her declarations, and even desired her to explain her precise parentage. The reader will remember that there had been an American marriage in Adrienne's family, and that every relative the poor girl had on earth was among these distant connections on this side of the Atlantic. One of these relatives, though it was no nearer than a third cousin, was Betts Shoreham, whose great-grandmother had been a bona fide de la Rocheaimard, and who was enabled, at once, to point out to the poor deserted orphan some forty or fifty persons who stood in the same degree of affinity to her. It is needless to say that this conversation was of absorbing interest to both; so much so, indeed, that Betts momentarily forgot his love, and by the time it had ended, Adrienne was disposed to overlook most of her over-scrupulous objections to rewarding that very passion. But the hour admonished them of the necessity of separating.

'And now, my beloved cousin,' said Betts Shoreham, as he rose to quit the room, seizing Adrienne's unresisting hand – 'now, my own Adrienne, you will no longer urge your sublimated notions of propriety against my suit. I am your nearest male relative, and have a right to your obedience – and I command that you be the second de la Rocheaimard who became the wife of a Shoreham.'

'Tell me, *mon cher cousin*,'[112] said Adrienne, smiling through her tears – 'were your grandparents, my good uncle and aunt, were they happy? Was their union blessed?'

'They were miracles of domestic felicity, and their happiness has passed down in tradition, among all their descendants. Even religion could not furnish them with a cause for misunderstanding. That example that they set to the last century, we will endeavor to set to this.'

Adrienne smiled, kissed her hand to Betts, and ran out of the room, leaving me forgotten on the sofa. Betts Shoreham seized his hat, and left the house, a happy man; for, though he had no direct promise as yet, he felt as reasonably secure of success, as circumstances required.

17

Five minutes later, Tom Thurston entered, and Julia Monson came down to receive *him*, her pique not interfering, and it being rather stylish to be disengaged on the morning of the day when the household was in all the confusion of a premeditated rout.

'This is so good of you, Miss Monson,' said Tom, as he made his bow – I heard it all, being still on the sofa – 'This is so good of you, when your time must have so many demands on it.'

'Not in the least, Mr. Thurston – mamma and the housekeeper have settled everything, and I am really pleased to see you, as you can give me the history of the new play – '

'Ah! Miss Monson, my heart – my faculties – my ideas – ' Tom was getting bothered, and he made a desperate effort to extricate himself – 'In short, my *judgment* is so confused and monopolized, that I have no powers left to think or speak of plays. In a word, I was not there.'

'That explains it, then – and what has thus confused your mind, Mr. Thurston?'

'The approach of this awful night. You will be surrounded by a host of admirers, pouring into your ears their admiration and love, and then what shall I have to support me, but that "yes," with which you once raised me from the depths of despair to an elevation of happiness that was high as the highest pinnacle of the caverns of Kentucky, raising me from the depths of Chimborazo.'[113]

Tom meant to reverse this image, but love is proverbially desperate in its figures of speech, and anything was better than appearing to hesitate. Nevertheless, Miss Monson was too well instructed, and had too much real taste, not to feel surprise at all this extravagance of diction and poetry.

'I am not certain, Mr. Thurston, that I rightly understand you,' she said. 'Chimborazo is not particularly low, nor are the caverns of Kentucky so strikingly elevated.'

'Ascribe it all to that fatal, heart-thrilling, hope-inspiring "yes," loveliest of human females,' continued Tom, kneeling with some caution, lest the straps of his pantaloons should give way – 'Impute all to your own lucid ambiguity, and to the torments of hope that I experience. Repeat that "yes," lovely, consolatory, imaginative being, and raise me from the thrill of depression, to the liveliest pulsations of all human acmes.'

'Hang it,' thought Tom, 'if she stand *that*, I shall presently be ashore. Genius itself can invent nothing finer.'

But Julia did stand it. She admired Tom for his exterior, but the admiration of no moderately sensible woman could overlook rodomontade so exceedingly desperate. It was trespassing too boldly on the proprieties to utter such nonsense to a gentlewoman, and Tom, who had got his practice in a very low school, was doomed to discover that he had overreached himself.

'I am not certain I quite understand you, Mr. Thurston,' answered the half-irritated, half-amused young lady; 'your language is so very extraordinary – your images so unusual – '

'Say, rather, that it is your own image, loveliest incorporation of perceptible incarnations,' interrupted Tom, determined to go for the whole, and recalling some rare specimens of magazine eloquence – 'Talk not of images, obdurate maid, when you are nothing but an image yourself.'

'I! Mr. Thurston – and of what is it your pleasure to accuse me of being the image?'

'O! unutterable wo – yes, inexorable girl, your vacillating "yes" has rendered me the impersonation of that oppressive sentiment, of which your beauty and excellence have become the mocking reality. Alas, alas! that bearded men,' – Tom's face was covered with hair – 'Alas, alas! that bearded men should be brought to weep over the contrarieties of womanly caprice.'

Here Tom bowed his head, and after a grunting sob or two, he raised his handkerchief in a very pathetic manner to his face, and thought to himself – 'Well, if she stand *that*, the Lord only knows what I shall say next.'

As for Julia, she was amused, though at first she had been a little frightened. The girl had a good deal of spirit, and she had *tant soit peu*[114] of mother Eve's love of mischief in her. She determined to 'make capital' out of the affair, as the Americans say, in shopkeeping slang.

'What is the "yes," of which you speak,' she inquired, 'and, on which you seem to lay so much stress?'

'That "yes" has been my bane and antidote,' answered Tom, rallying for a new and still more desperate charge. 'When first pronounced by your rubicund lips, it thrilled on my amazed senses like a beacon of light – '

'Mr. Thurston – Mr. Thurston – what *do* you mean?'

'Ah, d—n it,' thought Tom, 'I should have said "*humid* light" – how the deuce did I come to forget that word – it would have rounded the sentence beautifully.'

'What do I mean, angel of "humid light,"' answered Tom, aloud; 'I mean all I say, and lots of feeling besides. When the heart is anguished with unutterable emotion, it speaks in accents that deaden all the nerves, and thrill the ears.' Tom was getting to be animated, and when that was the case, his ideas flowed like a torrent after a thunder-shower, or in volumes, and a little muddily. 'What do I mean, indeed; I mean to have *you*,' he *thought*, 'and at least 80,000 dollars, or dictionaries, Webster's inclusive, were made in vain.'

'This is very extraordinary, Mr. Thurston,' rejoined Julia, whose sense of womanly propriety began to take the alarm; 'and I must insist on an explanation. Your language would seem to infer – really, I do not know, what it does *not* seem to infer. Will you have the goodness to explain what you mean by that "yes?"'

'Simply, loveliest and most benign of your sex, that once already, in answer to a demand of your hand, you deigned to reply with that energetic and encouraging monosyllable, yes – dear and categorical affirmative – ' exclaimed Tom, going off again at half-cock, highly impressed with the notion that rhapsody, instead of music, was the food of love – 'Yes, dear and categorical affirmative, with what ecstasy did not my drowsy ears drink in the melodious sounds – what extravagance of delight my throbbing heart echo its notes, on the wings of the unseen winds – in short, what considerable satisfaction your consent gave my pulsating mind!'

'Consent! – Consent is a strong *word*, Mr. Thurston!'

'It is, indeed, adorable Julia, and it is also a strong *thing*. I've known terrible consequences arise from the denial of a consent, not half as explicit as your own.'

'Consequences! – may I ask, sir, to what consequences you allude?'

'The consequences, Miss Monson – that is, the consequences of a violated troth, I mean – they may be divided into three parts – ' here, Tom got up, brushed his knees, each in succession, with his pocket handkerchief, and began to count on his fingers, like a lawyer who is summing up an argument – 'Yes, Miss Julia, into three parts. First come the pangs of unrequited love; on these I propose to enlarge presently. Next come the legal effects, always supposing that the wronged party can summon heart enough to carry on a suit, with bruised affections – '

'hang it,' thought Tom, 'why did I not think of that word "bruised" while on my knees; it would tell like a stiletto – ' 'Yes, Miss Julia, if "bruised affections" would permit the soul to descend to such pre-liminaries. The last consequence is, the despair of hope deferred.'

'All this is so extraordinary, Mr. Thurston, that I insist on knowing why you have presumed to address such language to me – yes, sir, *insist* on knowing your reason.'

Tom was dumbfounded. Now that he was up, and looking about him, he had an opportunity of perceiving that his mistress was offended, and that he had somewhat overdone the sublime, poetical and affecting. With a sudden revulsion of feeling and tactics, he determined to throw himself, at once, into the penitent and candid.

'Ah, Miss Monson,' he cried, somewhat more naturally – 'I see I have offended and alarmed you. But, impute it all to love. The strength of my passion is such, that I became desperate, and was resolved to try any expedient that I thought might lead to success.'

'That might be pardoned, sir, were it not for the extraordinary character of the expedient. Surely, you have never seen in me any taste for the very extraordinary images and figures of speech you have used, on this occasion.'

'This handkerchief,' – said Tom, taking me from the sofa – 'this handkerchief must bear all the blame. But for this, I should not have dreamt of running so much on the high-pressure principle; but love, you know, Miss Julia, is a calculation, like any other great event of life, and must be carried on consistently.'

'And, pray, sir, how can that handkerchief have brought about any such result?'

'Ah! Miss Monson, you ask me to use a most killing frankness! Had we not better remain under the influence of the poetical star?'

'If you wish to ensure my respect, or esteem, Mr. Thurston, it is necessary to deal with me in perfect sincerity. Nothing but truth will ever be pleasing to me.'

'Hang it,' thought Tom, again, 'who knows? She is whimsical, and may really like to have the truth. It's quite clear her heart is as insensible to eloquence and poetry as a Potter's Field wall, and it might answer to try her with a little truth. Your $80,000 girls get *such* notions in their heads, that there's no analogy, as one might say, between them and the rest of the species.' 'Miss Julia,' continuing aloud, 'my nature is all plain-dealing, and I am delighted to find a congenial spirit. You must have observed something very peculiar in my language, at the commencement of this exceedingly interesting dialogue?'

'I will not deny it, Mr. Thurston; your language was, to say the least, *very* peculiar.'

'Lucid, but ambiguous; pathetic, but amusing; poetical, but comprehensive; prosaical, but full of emphasis. That's my nature. Plain-dealing, too, is my nature, and I adore the same quality in others, most especially in those I could wish to marry.'

'Does this wish, then, extend to the plural number?' asked Julia, smiling a little maliciously.

'Certainly; when the heart is devoted to virtuous intentions, it wishes for a union with virtue, wherever it is to be found. Competence and virtue are my mottoes, Miss Julia.'

'This shows that you are, in truth, a lover of plain-dealing, Mr. Thurston – and now, as to the handkerchief?'

'Why, Miss Julia, perceiving that you are sincere, I shall be equally frank. You own this handkerchief?'

'Certainly, sir. I should hardly use an article of dress that is the property of another.'

'Independent, and the fruit of independence. Well, Miss Monson, it struck me that the mistress of such a handkerchief *must* like poetry – that is, flights of the imagination – that is, eloquence and pathos, as it might be engrafted on passion and sentiment.'

'I believe I understand you, sir; you wish to say that common sense seemed misapplied to the owner of such a handkerchief.'

'Far from that, adorable young lady; but that poetry, and eloquence, and flights of imagination, seem well applied. A very simple calculation will demonstrate what I mean. But, possibly, you do not wish to hear the calculation – ladies, generally, dislike figures?'

'I am an exception, Mr. Thurston; I beg you will lay the whole matter before me, therefore, without reserve.'

'It is simply this, ma'am. This handkerchief cost every cent of $100 – '

'One hundred and twenty-five,' said Julia quickly.

'Bless me,' thought Tom, 'what a rich old d—l her father must be. I will not give her up; and as poetry and sentiment do not seem to be favorites, here goes for frankness – some women are furious for plain matter-of-fact fellows, and this must be one of the number.' 'One hundred and twenty-five dollars is a great deal of money,' he added, aloud, 'and the interest, at 7 percent, will come to $1.75. Including first cost and washing, the annual expense of this handkerchief may be set down at $2. But the thing will not last now five years, if one includes fashion, wear and tear, &c., and this will bring the whole expense up to $27 per annum. We will suppose your fortune to be $50,000, Miss Julia – '

Here Tom paused, and cast a curious glance at the young lady, in the hope of hearing something explicit. Julia could hardly keep her countenance, but she was resolved to go to the bottom of all this plain-dealing.

'Well, sir,' she answered, 'we will suppose it, as you say, $50,000.'

'The interest, then, would be $3,500. Now 27 multiplied by 130 – ' here Tom took out his pencil and began to cipher – 'make just 3,510, or rather more than the whole amount of the interest. Well, when you come to deduct taxes, charges, losses and other things, the best invested estate of $3,500 per annum, will not yield more than $3,000, net. Suppose a marriage, and the husband has *only* $1,000 for his pocket, this would bring down the ways and means to $2,000 per annum; or less than a hundredth part of the expense of keeping *one* pocket handkerchief; and when you come to include rent, fuel, marketing, and other necessaries, you see, my dear Miss Monson, there is a great deal of poetry in paying so much for a pocket hand-kerchief.'

'I believe I understand you, sir, and shall endeavor to profit by the lesson. As I am wanted, you will now excuse me, Mr. Thurston – my father's step is in the hall – ' so Julia, in common with all other Manhattanese, called a passage, or entry, five feet wide – 'and to him I must refer you.'

This was said merely as an excuse for quitting the room. But Tom received it literally and figuratively, at the same time.

18

Accustomed to think of marrying as his means of advancement, he somewhat reasonably supposed 'refer you to my father' meant consent, so far as the young lady was concerned, and he determined to improve the precious moments. Fortunately for his ideas, Mr. Monson did not enter the room immediately, which allowed the gentleman an opportunity for a little deliberation. As usual, his thoughts took the direction of a mental soliloquy, much in the following form.

'This is getting on famously,' thought Tom. 'Refer you to my father – well, that is compact and comprehensive, at the same time. I wish her dandruff[115] had got up when I mentioned only $50,000. Seriously, that is but a small sum to make one's way on. If I had a footing of my own, in society, $50,000 *might* do; but, when a fellow has to work his way by means of dinners, horses, and et ceteras, it's a small allowance. It's true, the Monsons will give me connections, and connections are almost – not quite – as good as money to get a chap along with – but, the d—l of the matter is, that connections eat and drink. I dare say the Monson set will cost me a good $500 a year, though they will save something in the way of the feed they must give in their turns. I wish I had tried her with a higher figure, for, after all, it may have been only modesty – some women are as modest as the d—l. But here comes old Monson, and I must strike while the iron is hot.'

'Good morning, Mr. Thurston,' said the father, looking a little surprised at seeing such a guest at three o'clock. 'What, alone with my daughter's fine pocket handkerchief? You must find that indifferent company.'

'Not under the circumstances, sir. Everything is agreeable to us that belongs to an object we love.'

'Love? That is a strong term, Mr. Thurston – one that I hope you have uttered in pure gallantry.'

'Not at all, sir,' cried Tom, falling on his knees, as a schoolboy reads the wrong paragraph in the confusion of not having studied his lesson well – 'adorable and angelic – I beg your pardon, Mr. Monson,' – rising, and again brushing his knees with some care – 'my mind is in such a state of confusion, that I scarcely know what I say.'

'Really, I should think so, or you could never mistake me for a young girl of twenty. Will you have the goodness to explain this matter to me?'

'Yes, sir – I'm referred.'

'Referred? Pray, what may that mean in particular?'

'Only, sir, that I'm referred – I do not ask a dollar, sir. Her lovely mind and amiable person are all I seek, and I only regret that she is so rich. I should be the happiest fellow in the world, Mr. Monson, if the angelic Julia had not a cent.'

'The angelic Julia must be infinitely indebted to you, Mr. Thurston; but let us take up this affair in order. What am I to understand, sir, by your being referred?'

'That Miss Julia, in answer to my suit, has referred me to you, sir.'

'Then, so far as she herself is concerned, you wish me to understand that she accepts you?'

'Certainly – she accepted, some time since, with as heavenly a "yes" as ever came from the ruby lips of love.'

'Indeed! This is so new to me, sir, that you must permit me to see my daughter a moment, ere I give a definite answer.'

Hereupon Mr. Monson left the room, and Tom began to think again.

'Well,' he thought, 'things *do* go on swimmingly at last. This is the first time I could ever get at a father, though I've offered to six-and-twenty girls. One does something like a living business with a father. I don't know but I rather overdid it about the dollar, though it's according to rule to seem disinterested at first, even if you quarrel like furies, afterwards, about the stuff. Let me see – had I best begin to screw him up in this interview, or wait for the next? A few hints, properly thrown out, may be useful at once. Some of these old misers hold on to everything till they die, fancying it a mighty pleasant matter to chaps that can't support themselves to support *their* daughters by industry, as they call it. I'm as industrious as a young fellow can be, and I owe six months' board, at this very moment. No – no – I'll walk into him at once, and give him what Napoleon used to call a demonstration.'

The door opened, and Mr. Monson entered, his face a little flushed, and his eye a little severe. Still he was calm in tone and manner. Julia had told him all in ten words.

'Now, Mr. Thurston, I believe I understand this matter,' said the father, in a very businesslike manner; 'you wish to marry my daughter?'

'Exactly, sir; and she wishes to marry me – that is, as far as comports with the delicacy of the female bosom.'

'A very timely reservation. And you are referred?'

'Yes, Mr. Monson, those cheering words have solaced my ears – I am referred.' 'The old chap,' aside, 'likes a little humbug, as well as a girl.'

'And you will take her without a cent, you say?'

'Did I, sir? I believe I didn't exactly say that – *dollar* was the word I mentioned. *Cents* could hardly be named between you and me.'

'Dollar let it be, then. Now, sir, you have my consent on a single condition.'

'Name it, sir. Name five or six, at once, my dear Mr. Monson, and you shall see how I will comply.'

'One will answer. How much fortune do you think will be necessary to make such a couple happy, at starting in the world? Name such a sum as will comport with your own ideas.'

'How much, sir? Mr. Monson, you are a model of generosity! You mean, to keep a liberal and gentlemanly establishment, as would become your son-in-law?'

'I do – such a fortune as will make you both easy and comfortable.'

'Horses and carriages, of course? Every thing on a genteel and liberal scale?'

'On such a scale as will insure the happiness of man and wife.'

'Mutual esteem – conjugal felicity – and all that. I suppose you include dinners, sir, and a manly competition with one's fellow citizens, in real New York form?'

'I mean all that can properly belong to the expenses of a gentleman and lady.'

'Yes, sir – exceedingly liberal – liberal as the rosy dawn. Why, sir, meeting your proposition in the spirit in which it is offered, I should say Julia and I could get along very comfortably on $100,000. Yes, we could make that do, provided the money were well invested – no fancy stocks.'

'Well, sir, I am glad we understand each other so clearly. If my daughter really wishes to marry you, I will give $50,000 of this sum, as soon as you can show me that you have as much more to invest along with it.'

'Sir – Mr. Monson!'

'I mean that each party shall lay down dollar for dollar!'

'I understand what you mean, sir. Mr. Monson, that would be degrading lawful wedlock to the level of a bet – a game of cards – a mercenary, contemptible bargain. No, sir – nothing shall ever induce me to degrade this honorable estate to such pitiful conditions!'

'Dollar for dollar, Mr. Thurston!'

'Holy wedlock! It is violating the best principles of our nature.'

'Give and take!'

'Leveling the sacred condition of matrimony to that of a mere bargain for a horse or a dog!'

'Half and half!'

'My nature revolts at such profanation, sir – I will take $75,000 with Miss Julia, and say no more about it.'

'Equality is the foundation of wedded happiness, Mr. Thurston.'

'Say $50,000, Mr. Monson, and have no more words about it. Take away from the transaction the character of a bargain, and even $40,000 will do.'

'Not a cent that is not covered by a cent of your own.'

'Then, sir, I wash my hands of the whole affair. If the young lady should die, my conscience will be clear. It shall never be said Thomas Thurston was so lost to himself as to bargain for a wife.'

'We must, then, part, and the negotiation must fall through.'

Tom rose with dignity, and got as far as the door. With his hand on the latch, he added – 'Rather than blight the prospects of so pure and lovely a creature I will make every sacrifice short of honor – let it be $30,000, Mr. Monson?'

'As you please, sir – so that it be covered by $30,000 of your own.'

'My nature revolts at the proposition, and so – good morning, sir.'

Tom left the house, and Mr. Monson laughed heartily; so heartily, indeed, as to prove how much he relished the success of his scheme.

'Talk of Scylla and Charybdis!' soliloquized the discomfited Tom, as he wiped the perspiration from his face – 'Where the d—l does he think I am to find the $50,000 he wants, unless he first gives them to me? I never heard of so unreasonable an old chap! Here is a young fellow that offers to marry his daughter for $30,000 – half price, as one may say – and he talks about covering every cent he lays down with one of my own. I never knew what was meant by *cent percent* [116] before. Let me see; I've just thirty-two dollars and sixty-nine cents, and had we played at a game of coppers, I couldn't have held out half an hour. But, I flatter myself, I touched the old scamp up with morals, in a way he wasn't used to. Well, as this thing is over, I will try old Sweet, the grocer's daughter. If the wardrobe and whiskers fail there, I must rub up the Greek and Latin, and shift the ground to Boston. They say a chap with a little of the classics can get thirty or forty thousand, there, any day in the week. I wish my parents had brought me up a schoolmaster; I would be off in the first boat. Blast it! – I thought when I came down to $30,000, he would have snapped at the bait, like a pike. He'll never have a chance to get her off so cheap, again.'

This ended the passage of flirtation between Thomas Thurston and Julia Monson. As for the latter, she took such a distaste for me that she presented me to Mlle Hennequin, at the first opportunity, under the pretence that she had discovered a strong wish in the latter to possess me.

Adrienne accepted the present with some reluctance, on account of the price that had been paid for me, and yet with strong emotion. How she wept over me, the first time we were alone together! I thought her heart would break; nor am I certain it would not, but for the timely interposition of Julia, who came and set her laughing by a humorous narrative of what had occurred between her father and her lover.

That night the rout took place. It went off with éclat, but I did not make my appearance at it, Adrienne rightly judging that I was not a proper companion for one in her situation. It is true, this is not a very American notion, *every* thing being suitable for *every* body that get them, in this land of liberty, but Adrienne had not been educated in a land of liberty, and fancied that her dress should bear some relation to her means. Little did she know that I was a sort of patent of nobility, and that by exhibiting me, she might have excited envy, even in an alderman's daughter. My non-appearance, however, made no difference with Betts Shoreham, whose attentions throughout the evening were so marked as to raise suspicion of the truth in the mind of even Mrs. Monson.

The next day there was an éclaircissement. Adrienne owned who she was, gave my history, acquainted Mrs. Monson with her connection with Mr. Shoreham, and confessed the nature of his suit. I was present at this interview, and it would be unjust to say that the mother was not disappointed. Still she behaved generously, and like a high-principled woman. Adrienne was advised to accept Betts, and her scruples, on the score of money, were gradually removed, by Mrs. Monson's arguments.

'What a contrast do this Mr. Thurston and Adrienne present!' observed Mrs. Monson to her husband, in a tête-à-tête, shortly after this interview. 'Here is the gentleman wanting to get our child, without a shilling to bless himself with, and the poor girl refusing to marry the man of her heart, because she is penniless.'

'So much for education. We become mercenary or self-denying, very much as we are instructed. In this country, it must be confessed, fortune-hunting has made giant strides, within the last few years, and that, too, with an audacity of pretension that is unrestrained by any of the social barriers that exist elsewhere.'

'Adrienne will marry Mr. Shoreham, I think. She loves; and when a girl loves, her scruples of this nature are not invincible.'

'Aye, *he* can lay down dollar for dollar – I wish his fancy had run toward Julia.'

'It has not, and we can only regret it. Adrienne has half-consented, and I shall give her a handsome wedding – for, married she must be in our house.'

All came to pass as was predicted. One month from that day, Betts Shoreham and Adrienne de la Rocheaimard became man and wife. Mrs. Monson gave a handsome entertainment, and a day or two later, the bridegroom and bride took possession of their proper home. Of course I removed with the rest of the family, and, by these means, had an opportunity of becoming a near spectator of a honeymoon. I ought, however, to say, that Betts insisted on Julia's receiving $125 for me, accepting from Julia a handsome wedding present of equal value, but in another form. This was done simply that Adrienne might say when I was exhibited, that she had worked me herself, and that the lace with which I was embellished was an heirloom. If there are various ways of quieting one's conscience, in the way of marriage settlements, so are there various modes of appeasing our sense of pride.

Pocket handkerchiefs have their revolutions, as well as states. I was now under my first restoration, and perfectly happy; but, being French, I look forward to further changes, since the temperament that has twice ejected the Bourbons from their thrones will scarce leave me in quiet possession of mine forever.

Adrienne loves Betts more than anything else. Still she loves me dearly. Scarce a week passes that I am not in her hands; and it is when her present happiness seems to be overflowing that she is most fond of recalling the painful hours she experienced in making me what I am. Then her tears flow freely, and often I am held in her soft little hand, while she prays for the soul of her grandmother, or offers up praises for her own existing blessings. I am no longer thought of for balls and routs, but appear to be doomed to the closet, and those moments of tender confidence that so often occur between these lovers. I complain not. So far from it, never was an *article* of my character more highly favored, passing an existence, as it might be, in the very bosom of truth and innocence. Once only have I seen an old acquaintance, in the person of Clara Caverly, since my change of mistress – the idea of calling a de la Rocheaimard a *boss*, or *bossess*, is out of the question. Clara is a distant relative of Betts, and soon became intimate with her new cousin. One day she saw me lying on a table, and, after an examination, she exclaimed –

'Two things surprise me greatly here, Mrs. Shoreham – that *you* should own one of these *things*' – I confess I did not like the word – 'and that you should own this particular handkerchief.'

'Why so, *chère* Clara?' – how prettily my mistress pronounces that name; so different from *Clarry*!

'It is not like *you* to purchase so extravagant and useless a *thing* – and then this looks like a handkerchief that once belonged to another person – a poor girl who has lost her means of extravagance by the change of the times. But, of course, it is only a resemblance, as *you* – '

'It is more, Clara – the handkerchief is the same. But that handkerchief is not an article of dress with me; it is *my friend*!'

The reader may imagine how proud I felt! This was elevation for the species, and gave a dignity to my position, with which I am infinitely satisfied. Nevertheless, Miss Caverly manifested surprise.

'I will explain,' continued Mrs. Shoreham. 'The handkerchief is my own work, and is very precious to me, on account *des souvenirs*.'[117]

Adrienne then told the whole story, and I may say Clara Caverly became my friend also. Yes, she, who had formerly regarded me with indifference, or dislike, now kissed me, and wept over me, and in this manner have I since passed from friend to friend, among all of Adrienne's intimates.

Not so with the world, however. My sudden disappearance from it excited quite as much sensation as my debut in it. Tom Thurston's addresses to Miss Monson had excited the envy, and, of course, the attention of all the other fortune-hunters in town, causing his sudden retreat to be noticed. Persons of this class are celebrated for covering their retreats skillfully. Tom declared that 'the old chap broke down when they got as far as the fortune – that, as he liked the girl, he would have taken her with $75,000, but the highest offer he could get from him was $30,000. This, of course, no gentleman could submit to. A girl with such a pocket handkerchief *ought* to bring a clear $100,000, and I was for none of your halfway doings. Old Monson is a humbug. The handkerchief has disappeared, and, now they have taken down the *sign*, I hope they will do business on a more reasonable scale.'

A month later, Tom got married. I heard John Monson laughing over the particulars one day in Betts Shoreham's library, where I am usually kept, to my great delight, being exceedingly fond of books. The facts were as follows. It seems Tom had cast an eye on the daughter of a grocer of reputed wealth, who had attracted the attention of another person of his own school. To get rid of a competitor, this person pointed out to Tom a girl whose father had been a butcher, but had just retired from business, and was building himself a fine house some-where in Butcherland.

'That's your girl,' said the treacherous adviser. 'All butchers are rich, and they never build until their pockets are so crammed as to force them to it. They coin money, and spend nothing. Look how high beef has been of late years; and then they live on the smell of their own meats. This is your girl. Only court the old fellow, and you are sure of half a million in the long run.'

Tom was off on the instant. He did court the old fellow; got introduced to the family; was a favorite from the first; offered in a fortnight, was accepted, and got married within the month. Ten days afterward, the supplies were stopped for want of funds, and the butcher failed. It seems *he*, too, was only taking a hand in the great game of brag that most of the country had sat down to.

Tom was in a dilemma. He had married a butcher's daughter. After this, every door in Broadway and Bond street was shut upon him. Instead of stepping into society on his wife's shoulders, he was dragged out of it by the skirts, through her agency. Then there was not a dollar. His empty pockets were balanced by her empty pockets. The future offered a sad perspective. Tom consulted a lawyer about a divorce, on the ground of 'false pretences.' He was even ready to make an affidavit that he had been slaughtered. But it would not do. The marriage was found to stand all the usual tests, and Tom went to Texas.

NOTES

1. The Latin name of the variety of flax that is used to make linen and linseed oil.
2. Irish. After Milesius, legendary ancestor of the Irish.
3. Town in Normandy.
4. A noble family from Languedoc, southern France.
5. Future (French).
6. Mind, spirit (French).
7. 'Rotting' (or 'retting') is the process of soaking flax in water, to soften it in preparation for weaving. Its fibers are then separated out by beating, which is probably what Cooper means by 'crackling.'
8. Combed, the final stage of preparing the flax for weaving.
9. Marie Thérèse d'Angoulême (1778–1851), the only daughter of Louis XVI.
10. Open spaces where new linen is stretched out on the ground to whiten in the sun.
11. *Legitimist*: a royalist who supported the claims of the representative of the senior line of the house of Bourbon to be the legitimate king of France. Leftist *liberals* argued for reform.
12. 'Left side' liberals and 'right side' *legitimists* (French).
13. '"Nazareth! Can anything good come from there?"' (John 1:46).
14. Center left (French).
15. Marie Amélie (1782–1866), daughter of King Ferdinand IV of Naples, sister of King Francis I of The Two Sicilies. She became queen when her husband the Duke of Orleans seized the throne from Charles X on 31st July 1830.
16. Marie Caroline (1798–1870), wife of Charles Ferdinand of Artois, Duke of Berry, second son of King Charles X.
17. Lady's maid.
18. Shop (French).
19. Custom house (French).
20. Courier (French).
21. Most useful (Latin).
22. Dear me!; good heavens!; my oh my! (French).
23. King of France 1774–93; he was guillotined following the Revolution of 1789.
24. General commanding a brigade.
25. The good old days (French).
26. For the time being (French).
27. Council of relatives, supervised by a judge (French).
28. Village priest (French).
29. My friend (French).
30. Wedding presents (French).
31. Gold coin minted in the reign of Napoleon I, equal to twenty francs.
32. Perfect (French).
33. Neighborhood (French).

34. The Duchesse d' Angoulême (see note 9).

35. Gossip (French).

36. Four decrees establishing absolute rule, issued by King Charles X on 25th July 1830, which touched off the July Revolution.

37. Good area (French).

38. There are Bourbons and there are Bourbons (French).

39. New Year's Day (French).

40. Sulking, silent (French).

41. French banker and politician (1767–1844).

42. Stock exchange (French).

43. Stockbrokers (French).

44. Small coin (five centimes); twenty sous are equal to one franc.

45. Pawnbrokers.

46. Dining-room (French).

47. Milliner (French).

48. Cunning (French).

49. Seamstress (French).

50. A young working-class woman.

51. 'A thimble, young lady!' (French).

52. Never (French).

53. However (French).

54. Ground or first floor (French).

55. Word of honor (French).

56. Private income (French).

57. Half-farthing (French).

58. Cortege (French).

59. A paraphrase of Hebrews 12:6, 'For whom the Lord loveth he chasteneth, and scourgeth every son whom he receiveth.'

60. In the next edition of the magazine.

61. Reserve corps (French).

62. A pocket handkerchief (French).

63. Gently (French).

64. Number 120 (French).

65. Trunk (French).

66. Of the American national guard (French).

67. Boys, waiters (French).

68. Living room, parlor (French).

69. The 1832 American Tariff Act, which had high customs duties on the import of textile products.

70. Customs officials (French).

71. Eugène François Vidocq (1775–1857), a French criminal turned informer, then detective.

72. Pupil (French).

73. Box (French).

74. Learned people.

75. An archaic exclamation derived from 'In faith.'

76. Always the same (Latin). The shirt is presumably being ironic.

77. 'To the manner born,' from *Hamlet*, 1.4.14ff, frequently misquoted as 'to the manor born.'

78. Supporter of King Charles X.

79. Ever so little of (French).

80. My dear (French).

81. Stupid or inane remarks (French).

82. As a connoisseur (French).

83. 'Was out' – had been presented to society.

84. In 1786 William Pitt the Younger (1759–1806) introduced a sinking fund to underpin national finances.

85. 'Fetch me the handkerchief,' from Shakespeare's *Othello*, 1.4.98.

86. Discretion (French).

87. Dining-room parlors (French).

88. Claude Lorrain (1600–82), French landscape painter; Thomas Cole (1801–48), painter who was born in Britain and emigrated to the United States, and founded the Hudson River school of landscape painting.

89. In 1833 Andrew Jackson (1767–1845), seventh President of the United States (1829–37) moved the federal government's deposits from the Second Bank of the United States, triggering a brief financial panic.

90. Dandies (French).

91. Female colleagues (French).

92. See note 89.

93. Sir Walter Scott (1771–1832), British novelist and poet.

94. In private (Italian).

95. Princely (French).

96. Naturally, it being understood (French).

97. The Corso is a main street in Rome.

98. Too much, one too many (French).

99. Good taste (French).

100. In passing (French).

101. Diplomats (French).

102. Alexis de Tocqueville (1805–59) was a French political thinker and historian. After spending time in the United States he published *Democracy in America* (1835, 1840).

103. A handkerchief is Iago's means of fueling Othello's suspicions of his wife Desdemona, in Shakespeare's play *Othello*. See also note 85.

104. Poem by Thomas Moore (1779–1852), Irish poet.

105. Devoted (French).

106. Ancient Greco-Roman city in Italy.

107. (Musical) scales (French).

108. Lady Mary Wortley Montagu (1689–1762), poet, essayist, and feminist.

109. Paris Opera House.

110. Gouverneur Morris (1752–1816), American statesman. Pinckney's Treaty allowed the United States free navigation of the Mississippi River and to deposit goods at New Orleans without paying customs duties.

111. See notes 85 and 103.

112. My dear cousin (French).

113. Volcano in Ecuador.

114. A little bit (French).

115. Tom confuses the words 'dander' and 'dandruff' – their primary meaning is the same, but 'dander' can also mean 'temper,' while 'dandruff' cannot.

116. One hundred percent.

117. Of memories (French).

BIOGRAPHICAL NOTE

James Fenimore Cooper was born in New Jersey in 1789, the eleventh of twelve children. When he was a year old his family moved to the frontier of Otsego Lake, New York, where his father established a settlement that became Cooperstown, New York.

Cooper was schooled at Albany and New Haven, and attended Yale College for two years before being expelled in 1805 for a dangerous prank. He joined the United States Navy but resigned his commission in 1811 following his marriage to Susan Augusta de Lancey. They settled in Westchester County, New York, and Cooper embarked upon his prolific literary career.

His first novel, *Precaution*, was published anonymously in 1820, and was followed in 1821 by the very successful *The Spy*. In 1823 he wrote *The Pioneers*, the first of his *Leatherstocking Tales*, a series of five historical romances featuring the frontiersman Natty Bumppo. *The Pilot* and *Lionel Lincoln* followed in 1824 and 1825 respectively, and in 1826 Cooper published the second in the *Leatherstocking* series, the epic novel *The Last of the Mohicans*, which many take to be his masterpiece. Despite its flaws it was one of the most popular English-language novels of its day, and it established Cooper as a world-famous writer.

Cooper left the United States for Paris, where in 1826 he published *The Prairie*, another strong work in the *Leatherstocking* series. He continued to write at a rate of about one novel a year, and became increasingly involved in political controversies. These influenced his writing; between 1831 and 1833 he wrote three novels that had a strong republican sentiment.

He returned to America in 1833, where his increasingly political and defensive writings earned him some bad feeling. Cooper returned to writing novels in 1839, and his work from this period includes the last two *Leatherstocking Tales*, *The Pathfinder* in 1840 and *The Deerslayer* in 1841. *Autobiography of a Pocket Handkerchief* was published in 1843. He continued writing until 1850.

Cooper spent the last years of his life in Cooperstown, where he died in September 1851.